LOVE AND GLORY

Books by Robert B. Parker

THE GODWULF MANUSCRIPT
GOD SAVE THE CHILD
MORTAL STAKES
PROMISED LAND
THREE WEEKS IN SPRING (with Joan Parker)
THE JUDAS GOAT
WILDERNESS
LOOKING FOR RACHEL WALLACE
EARLY AUTUMN
A SAVAGE PLACE
CEREMONY
THE WIDENING GYRE
LOVE AND GLORY

LOVE
AND
GLORY

Robert B. Parker

Delacorte Press / Seymour Lawrence

"As Time Goes By": words and music by Herman Hupfeld.
Copyright © 1931 (renewed) Warner Bros., Inc. All rights reserved.
Used by permission.

Published by
Delacorte Press/Seymour Lawrence
1 Dag Hammarskjold Plaza
New York, N.Y. 10017

MANUFACTURED IN THE UNITED STATES OF AMERICA
FIRST PRINTING

LIBRARY OF CONGRESS CATALOGING IN PUBLICATION DATA
Parker, Robert B., 1932–
    Love and glory

    I. Title.
PS3566.A686L68   1983   813'.54   83–1987
ISBN 0-385-29261-9

FOR JOAN: *"We all try. You succeed."*

PROLOGUE

It's still the same old story,
A fight for love and glory,
A case of do or die.
The fundamental things apply
As time goes by.

CHAPTER
ONE

In memory it seems someone else, a boy in a glen plaid
suit and a lime green shirt chewing gum with a cigarette
behind his ear while he danced awkwardly with a girl
who made his stomach buzz, and Frankie Laine sang
"Black Lace" on the record player. But it wasn't someone
else, it was me, or at least the beginning of me. It was the
evening I was born: an embryonic kid with his hair
slicked back, I danced, for the first time, with Jennifer
Grayle; and the flowering of my soul was forever wed to
a vision of possibility so gorgeous and unspeakable that
even now it seems a trick of time and memory. No child
could have felt what I felt. And yet . . . the buzz in my
stomach has buzzed for thirty years and buzzes still, an
implacable thrill of passion and purpose that has galva-
nized me like the touch of God's finger on Adam's inert
hand.

As we danced at that freshman dance in the early fall
of 1950, it was as if the still serpentless meadows of Eden
spread out around us. We are east of Eden now, full of

knowledge. We know that lambs and lions will not gambol, if they ever did, in a green eternity. But we know much more than that, and some of what we know is worth mortality.

I had gone from an unaffluent city up to Colby College in September of 1950, virginal, full of fantasy, and nearly devoid of social graces, to major in English and become a writer. I wasn't scared. I'd been away before. I knew I'd make friends, but I was frightened of girls and the freshman dance made me anxious. None of us knew one another yet. We had no gang to hang with in a corner, to play to as we danced. No one whose approval we had tested and could count on. My name tag, pinned to my wide lapels, said HI, MY NAME'S BOONE ADAMS, WHAT'S YOURS? Wearing it made me feel like a perfect asshole, but everyone was wearing theirs.

She was wearing a black dress and there was a sort of richness about her, a density of presence that made her seem more tangible than other people. At eighteen I thought she looked sexy. Chewing three sticks of Juicy Fruit, I swaggered over and asked her to dance. Bravado.

She danced as badly as I did. We were barely able to maneuver the floor.

She said, "Are you enjoying Colby so far?"

"Yeah, sure, it's okay," I said. "Where you from?"

"Marblehead, Mass."

I danced as close as I could. I thought it was a way to make out. Her thighs moved against me, and I could feel the faint masking slickness of her slip.

"Yeah?" I said. "I know a guy in Marblehead. Moved there from New Bedford. Frankie Gonsalves. You know him?"

"I don't think so," she said. I pressed a little harder against her. "What does his father do?"

"His old man's dead," I said. "His old lady works in a fish market, I think. He's a real hot shit."

She didn't cringe at the swear word. Did that mean she'd come across? I'd always harbored the hope that girls who swore also screwed.

"I don't think I know him," she said. "Did he go to Marblehead High?"

"I think he dropped out."

"Oh."

The record ended. We stood for a moment. Then she said, "Well, thank you very much. I hope we'll get to know each other better."

"Yeah, maybe we should grab a few beers together sometime, huh?"

"Yes, that would really be fun," she said. And then she walked back to the side of the room where the girls congregated. I walked back and stood among the boys I didn't know yet. I took the cigarette from behind my ear and put it in the corner of my mouth and snapped a paper match with one hand and lit the cigarette. I leaned my back against the wall with my hands in my pockets, and hooked my right heel over the molding ledge, and smoked my cigarette without taking it from my mouth. Cool.

My thighs felt thick and hot where hers had brushed them and the light and only occasional touch of her lower belly against me as we danced seemed now to continue. I thought about her looking up at me in the moonlight with her eyes slitted and her mouth half open, her arms around my neck her head thrown back her breath smell-

ing of champagne; a soft wind that smelled of distant vio-
lets stirred her hair. Across the room I saw her being
asked to dance. She smiled and went to the floor with a
tall kid from Long Island whose name I didn't know. He
knew how to dance.

I watched her looking up at him and smiling. I
should have asked her again. Maybe after this number. I
could feel myself shrinking inside. She moved about the
floor with the kid from Long Island. The music ended.
He said something, she laughed, and he left her with the
girls. NOW. *Hi, Jennifer, care to try it again?* The new
record came on. Something by Les Brown and His Band
of Renown. Several of the girls she was with went to the
dance floor. She was alone for a moment; she looked
around. NOW. Why not now? She moved toward another
group of girls. I lit a new cigarette in the corner of my
mouth and walked slowly out of the room and back
across the campus with the smoke stinging my eyes and
my stomach knotted with something like fear and something like grief. The dark sky was very very high and I
was very far from home and very very small.

CHAPTER
TWO

The cinder block classroom reeked with heat. The windows were closed. The radiator hissed. Mr. Crosbie, the instructor, was outlining a successful expository essay on the board.

"We begin," he said, "with the topic sentence." He wrote I. TOPIC SENTENCE on the blackboard.

"Now, in Cardinal Newman's essay that you read for today, what is the topic sentence?"

I was reading Mr. Crosbie's comments on my first paper. "A certain weak humor," he'd scribbled, "and the suggestion of imaginative reach. But riddled with punctuation errors, run-ons, and sentence frags. It is inappropriate to a formal expository essay." A large red F was circled at the bottom.

Two seats away from me to my right, Jennifer Grayle was sitting. I had passed her in the corridor on the way to class and she had ignored me. I had bitten off my anxious *hello* just in time when I realized she wasn't going to speak. Maybe she didn't mean the stuff about getting to know me better. Now she was sitting with her textbook open to Newman's essay and her pencil poised to underline the topic sentence as soon as someone identified it.

"Well, what is the essay about," Crosbie was saying.

Jennifer was wearing a black woolen shirt and faded blue jeans with the cuffs turned up. The jeans were smooth over her buttocks and thighs. I looked at them and felt my abdominal muscles clench like a fist. *Christ she looked right through me when I went to say hello. Right fucking through me.*

The steam pipes that fed the big iron radiator gave a chunk. I looked at the F on my first college theme. My stomach had the going-down-in-an-elevator feeling it always got when I'd been caught.

Mr. Crosbie wasn't making much progress. He shook his head. "I don't think one can say that the topic of the essay is religion. You need to be more specific."

Jennifer's hair was dark brown with now and then a glint in it, sort of a copperish glint. It came to her shoulders and then turned up slightly. Her lower lip was full and her mouth was wide. Where the black woolen shirt opened at the throat I could see, from my angle, the hint of her white breast.

My face felt hot. I was wearing a gray Orlon pullover shirt and it itched against my back. I shifted a little in the yellow-maple chair. On the writing arm there were initials engraved with hard-tipped pencils, some of them quite ornate. Some of them childish. A lot of the initials were designs where the letters were incorporated into each other, a B on the second leg of a capital R, things like that. A number of the initials were of couples. RP & JH. Occasionally they were in hearts.

I looked at the watch on the wrist of a guy next to me. 8:20. Jesus, class lasted till 9:00. I couldn't last. My eyes kept closing and when they closed my head would begin to sag forward and then jerk back as I caught myself. I shifted in my chair again. My underwear was damp with sweat and felt too tight. I looked at Jennifer. She didn't look hot. I wouldn't think about her underwear, or sweat. I knew that the laws of nature required her to have many of the same bodily functions I did, but that was only technically true. My imagination never accepted it as real.

Mr. Crosbie was getting mad, or desperate. "What do you think an expository essay is?" he said. The class, wretched in its hot boredom, coalesced into mute submission. I gave up. With my feet propped on the empty chair next to me, I tipped my own chair back against the wall, folded my arms across my chest, and let my head relax forward.

Mr. Crosbie was leaning forward over his lecture table looking at his seating plan. "Mr. Franklin," he said, "define exposition."

Franklin was hunched over his notebook and text, staring at them blankly. The more he looked the more they didn't tell him what exposition meant.

"Mr. Franklin?"

Franklin was very ivy with his oxford button-down and chinos. He wore his blond hair in a crew cut, and his white bucks looked pre-scuffed. He was in college on some kind of church-related scholarship. He looked up finally from the unobliging textbook and said, "I'm sorry, sir. I'm afraid I don't know."

Crosbie said, without looking up from his seating chart, "I'm afraid you don't. Miss Grayle, do you know?"

I felt a little thrill in the delta of my breastbone when he said her name. She sat up straight and looked right at him, but I could see the faint flush of embarrassment darken her face.

"It's a kind of story that's true," she said.

Crosbie smiled without humor, "Oh," he said, "really? What kind of a story exactly?"

Jennifer said, "Not a story that's been made up." She gestured slightly with one hand.

Crosbie placed both hands on his little lectern and leaned over it, looked straight at Jennifer.

"Miss Grayle," he said, and let the name hang there in the stifling room. He shook his head. "Miss Grayle, an essay is not a story. It may or may not be about something that, as you so cleverly put it, 'is made up.' Mr. Franklin's answer revealed that he didn't know, but yours reveals *how much* you didn't know." His eyes swept the room. Jennifer looked down at her book. Crosbie's eyes settled on me, slouched in the back. He checked his seating plan.

"Mr. Adams," he said. "If I'm not disturbing your rest, can you define expository for us."

"If an old man shows himself to a little girl in the playground," I said, "that's an expository act. If he writes it up after, it's probably an expository essay."

Billy Murphy, sitting in the other back corner of the room, burst out a loud "Haw." Everyone else was silent. Crosbie's face got red. He looked at me. I looked back. I could feel anxiety and anger mingling in my gut. I was still tilted back with my feet up.

Crosbie said, "I think we've had enough of you in this class for today, Mr. Adams. You may leave."

I shrugged, let my chair tip slowly forward, closed my book and notebook with exaggerated care, took the unlighted Camel cigarette from behind my ear, stuck it in my mouth, and walked slowly toward the front of the room. I looked down at Jennifer as I went by, and her eyes glinted with sharp, repressed humor. She understood what I'd done. It made my back tingle.

"Promptly"—Crosbie glanced down at the seating chart—"Mr. Adams."

At the door I stopped, looked at Crosbie, and said, "The thing is, my answer was right."

Then I looked at the class, made a short wave to Billy Murphy, whose face was bunched with amusement, and walked out. I left the door open behind me.

CHAPTER
THREE

I looked at myself in the mirror back of Onie's bar. Five foot ten inches, weight 160 pounds, hair medium brown, crew cut, complexion fair, some acne. Whiskers, none to speak of. I didn't like the acne much, nor the lack of beard. Lots of my buddies had dark heavy beards and shaved daily. I sucked on my cigarette, holding it between my thumb and middle finger.

The bartender said, "You ready yet, Boonie?"

I nodded. He took my glass, drew another beer into it, and put it back. "Fresh barrel, Boonie, you'll like it."

I grinned. "Thanks, Reenie."

In two months I'd made some progress. I was first name with the bartender at Onie's and at school I was already on the dean's other list. The smoke in Onie's was fog thick, and it eddied in the narrow crowded room as people went to and from the rest rooms and shifted about in the booths. Someone played "Mixed Emotions" on the jukebox and I tried to listen through the noise that was as thick and eddied as the smoke. It was the Rosemary

Clooney version, not Ella's, and I liked it better, although it made me feel disloyal.

"Hey, Boonie, I hear you got bounced out of soc class?"

"Just for the day," I said.

"You shoulda seen it, Pat. Boonie was passed out in the back with a bad hangover and old Schlossberg says to him 'Mr. Adams, do you mind if I interrupt your rest for just a moment?' And Boonie's got his eyes still closed and he says 'Yes.'"

"Honest to God? Booner, you are a hot shit, I'll give you that. So did Schlossie kick you out?"

I nodded.

"You're never going to make it, Boonie. You won't last the year, never mind four."

In the mirror I saw Jennifer come in with a date. It was the tall kid from Long Island she'd danced with the first night I'd seen her. His name was Taylor and he was supposed to be the best basketball player ever to come out of Douglaston High School. I drank the rest of my beer and gestured at René. He drew another and put it before me, took a dime from the change on the bar in front of me, winked, made a sort of clicking sound out of the corner of his mouth, and moved down the bar. I lit another Camel in the corner of my mouth and let the smoke drift up past my eyes. Through it I watched Jennifer in the mirror. She took off her camel's-hair coat and Taylor hung it on the hanger by the booth. She was wearing a white cashmere sweater and a Black Watch plaid skirt. When she slid into the booth I saw her thigh for a moment. Taylor said something, and she put her head back and laughed. I couldn't hear the sound of her laugh across the boisterous room, but her face colored slightly with it. I'd already noticed that when she laughed she flushed slightly. I had already noticed, too, that her mouth was slightly crooked. Her upper and lower lip did not center exactly.

"Hey, Nick Taylor's going out with Jennifer Grayle?"

"Yeah, since the homecoming dance. I'd like to get a piece of that, uh, Guze?"

"I'd like to go over right now and take a big fucking bite out of one of those thighs. How about it, Boonze, you like some of that?"

Their voices came sifting through the smoke as if they were in another room. I looked at them.

"Want to get into Jenny Grayle, Boonie? I'll bet Taylor's getting his share."

The smoke swirled and thickened and mixed with the noise until I felt enclosed in a kind of transsensual element of which my own soul was but an inlet.

I shrugged. "But how much beer can she drink," I said.

"I thought she was going with Dave Herman."

"She's gone steady with three guys already this year."

I watched her in the mirror. Her hands resting quietly on the table, her head forward slightly, her eyes on Taylor's face. Taylor tapped each of her fingernails with the tip of his index finger. She smiled. Her beer was barely touched. I knew she didn't drink much, although it was said that she did. But she didn't. The music changed on the jukebox. Billy Eckstine, "I Apologize."

"What're you doing about that short story, Guze?"

"I'm getting my buddy Boone here to churn one out. How many you written so far this semester, Boonie?"

"Twenty-two," I said. "It's the dumbest fucking thing I ever heard of, making the whole freshman class write a fucking short story."

"You write one for me, Boonie?"

I nodded. "So far I got a B average. It woulda been higher, but Billy Murphy rewrote the one I did for him and got an F."

"How much you want?"

I made a rejecting wave with my left hand. "You can buy me a few beers some night."

"You got an A on yours, Boonie?"

"Yeah. Really piss me off if I got a worse mark on the one I handed in than the other twenty-one."

"You think they'll get wise? How about Guze passes in a terrific short story? Think they might get suspicious? Guze can't even fucking talk."

Jennifer had shifted in the booth and had her feet tucked up under her, sitting half sideways. She was smoking a Pall Mall with the red crescent of her lipstick impressed on the tip. Taylor walked two fingers along the back of her left hand and up her arm as it lay on the table. Then he said something and got up and walked to the men's room.

"Hey, Boonie, how about the time you wrote a paper for Jackovich and Markham calls him in and asks him to explain it. Jackie about shit. Did he read it even before he handed it in?"

"Jackie can't read," I said. "You know that."

Jennifer took a compact from her purse, opened it,

and looked at herself in the small mirror. She turned her head a little to the left and then a little to the right, tilting the mirror to get the overhead light. She took a small gold tube from her purse and applied more lipstick, then looked again in the mirror, touched it up slightly, touched her hair in several places.

"What happened to him?"

"Markham flunked him."

"You shouldn't sound so smart, Boonie."

"I try, Guze. But I can't sound as dumb as Jackie, for crissake."

Taylor, on his way back from the men's room, looked over at me and said, "Hey, Boonie, come over and sit down. I'll buy you a beer."

A sharp sensation flashed up from my buttocks and tightened my throat. I sucked in half my Camel and held the smoke in my lungs and then blew it out the way you blow out a candle. My beer glass was empty. I picked up my cigarettes and walked over toward the booth where Jennifer sat.

CHAPTER
FOUR

I slid into the booth on Taylor's side. "I'll sit with you, Nick, so your date won't be all over me."

"You know Jennifer, Boonie?"

"Seen her around," I said. "Aren't you in my English class?"

"Mr. Crosbie?"

"Yeah, that's where I've seen you. When I make it." I lit a cigarette. "Which is not often. Unless something goes wrong I still have a hangover at eight in the morning."

"I remember you quite well." Jennifer's eyes glinted again. "So does Crosbie. How is he treating you these days?"

"I got an F on my first paper, but after that I've done okay."

"What you gotta understand is that Boonie's smart as a bastard," Nick Taylor said. "I know he don't look it, but he is. Did you have to write a short story for English?"

"Yes," Jennifer said. "Wasn't it awful."

"Boonie wrote half the ones in the freshman class. How many'd you write, Boonie?"

"Twenty-two," I said, "but who counts."

"Do you want to be a writer?" Jennifer said. She looked really interested. The way she had when I danced with her, as if what I said really mattered.

"Yes," I said.

"It's not something you can just interview for, is it. Does the uncertainty scare you?"

"I don't know, I guess so. But you have to assume you can make it, I guess, or you wouldn't try."

"What do you want to do besides write?" Jennifer said.

"Drink beer," I said. *And lie beside you in a spring meadow forever.*

She laughed, "And you're down here practicing." She was interested. "Would you want to work at a newspaper, or in advertising?"

"I don't know. I don't think I could stand the office and briefcase bit. I don't want nine to five for the rest of my life in some goddamned white clapboard suburb." *Unless with you. I'd do anything to be with you.* "I thought I might write the great American novel."

Jennifer puffed on her Pall Mall. There was reserved appraisal in her eyes. Nick held her hand across the table. "I hope you do," she said.

"I'm a business major," Taylor said. "I'd like to get into sales, work my way up to sales management maybe."

Her attention shifted from me to him and I could feel slackness, a kind of ebbing, as Taylor traced small patterns on the back of her hand. Mixed with the smoke and the malt smell of spilled beer, her perfume persisted, and as I became aware of it, the smell of it overpowered everything else. I felt disseminated, as if I eddied, commingling with her sound and the smell of her in the loud and smoky room.

Nick looked at his watch. "Better get you back, love," he said to Jennifer. "You have to be in in an hour and we need some time for parking, right?"

She smiled. "Good to see you, my dear," she said to me. "Maybe I'll see you in Bing's class someday."

"Tell him to sing 'When the Blue of the Night Meets the Gold of the Day' for me. I might come for that."

Jennifer laughed. She and Nick got up to go out. As they edged down the narrow, crowded aisle between the booths, Nick patted her companionably on the fanny. She looked back at me and winked and then leaned her head against Nick's shoulder. Get up to the campus for a little make-out time. The press of her wide mouth, the taste of her lipstick, the smell of cigarette smoke faintly mingled with beer on her breath. Her perfume. The tousle of her hair. The smell of fresh autumn air about her . . . with Nick; but there had been the wink and the moment of shared knowledge. Knowledge of what I didn't yet know.

I was alone in the booth, smoking my cigarette. Her glass with the lipstick circle on the rim stood three-quarters full across from me. I took in a lungful of smoke and picked up her glass and drank the rest of her beer. Then I let the smoke out slowly and watched it drift and eddy and disappear into the larger haze of the barroom.

CHAPTER
FIVE

We were in the spa drinking coffee and smoking and I was explaining a poem.

"Think about it," I said. "Why worms?"

"Which line is that," Billy Murphy said.

"Down here," I said, "line twenty-seven."

"My echoing song then worms shall try that long preserved virginity," Nick Taylor said, running the words and lines together without pause or comprehension.

"A worm's gonna screw her?" Guze said.

"Screw who?" Billy said.

"I don't know, this is some sick poem, Boonie. A worm screwing a virgin?"

"It's about you. You'd screw a worm, Guze, if some-one would hold it."

"Yeah, but I ain't no virgin."

"So you say."

"Shut up," I said. "You want to pass this fucking test or not?"

"Yeah. How much time we got?"

"Hour and a half."

I saw Jennifer across the spa. She was barely visible talking with three girls in another booth. The ripe thrust of her lower lip and part of her chin were all that showed among the other heads in the booth. I shifted a little and caught her eye. She smiled. I winked at her. There were six of us crowded into my booth and the smoke was thick. It is hard to think of that time now without seeing it through the glower of cigarette smoke that hung in hot, crowded places.

"C'mon, Boonie, explain the goddamn poem, will you?"

"He's saying if you wait too long to come across, you'll die and then the worms will eat you in the grave."

"Jeez, what a nice poem," Billy Murphy said.

I shrugged. "And he says worms, rather than, say, ants, which also eat corpses, because a worm is like a schwantz, you know. It's an appropriate image."

Nick Taylor said, "Wait a minute. Wait just a fucking minute. I know what that is. That's a goddamned phallic symbol."

I nodded.

"Sym-bo-lism," Guze said, dragging the word out. "Symbo-fucking-lism."

"Terrific, Guze. Put that down on your exam."

"Are you shitting? In the exam I'm going to cheat off of Boonie."

"You better."

Jennifer was looking at us. Nick Taylor, I suppose. She could hear most of the talk because she was close. But everyone knew she wasn't bothered by swearing.

"Before that," Billy Murphy said, "what's this shit about a chariot?"

Jennifer took her cigarette from her mouth and flicked the ashes onto the floor outside her booth with a shake of her hand. There was a wonderful carelessness about her. A kind of arrogant disinterest in some of the most elementary proprieties, the way I always imagined a princess might act, first in line to the throne, adored by the king and queen, worshipped by the people, she could shake the ash from her cigarette without looking where it would land. She could do whatever she wanted. Her wanting it made it right. And yet she was very polite, she always called professors sir. She dressed exactly the way she should; she was always a complete expression of the received look at Colby in 1950. Exactly sloppy enough, exactly enough makeup, exactly right roll in the cuffs of her jeans. It would have confused me in someone else, this seeming discontinuity, both careless and careful, but I applied no mortal categories to her. I saw her in great detail, and clearly, but I saw her as if through a projected overlay, which imposed upon the real contours of her attraction, the ornate illuminations of my dream. It was as if a real person had walked in the path of a movie projector. My imagination played upon her face until the reality was neither she nor the projection, but the fusion of both. In those days, just turned eighteen, her carelessness seemed to me, breathless in adoration, the identifying gesture of breeding and style. She was never careless with me.

"Boonie, what's this fucking chariot? If I flunk this test, they'll draft my ass."

"In a lot of classical myths and stuff the sun was seen to ride across the sky in a chariot," I said. "And so Marvell uses it to suggest time."

"What's time got to do with the sun?"

"The sun is the basis of time. Why the Christ do you think there's twenty-four hours in a day?"

"Oh, yeah. Why the hell doesn't he just say it?"

I shrugged. "The idea of a chariot bearing down on the two lovers is also threatening, you know, like a war chariot."

Billy Murphy said, "Guze, don't try to figure it out, just remember it."

"Whyn't they have us read stuff we can understand?"

"If you understood it, what would the fucking English teachers do every day in class?" I said.

"I'm going to work the meat counter at my old man's market when I graduate," Billy Murphy said. "I wonder what good Crosbie thinks this will do me."

"Liberalize your views of life," I said. "Make you a better human."

"Like Crosbie?"

"Yeah. That'd be good in the market, huh?" I put on a fruity accent. "Perhaps a slice of boiled ham, madam?"

The laughter rolled around the table. In the booth behind us I saw Jennifer smile. Her mouth was wide and bright when she smiled, making a broad crimson slash across her face. Her front teeth were white and slightly uneven, one of the canines barely out of line. The effect of the laughter on her face was to emphasize her cheekbones.

Nick Taylor said, "Come on, come on, we only got an

hour left. How about this next poem? How do you pronounce the guy's name?"

"Donne," I said, "rhymes with gun."

"Jesus, why doesn't he spell it right?"

"Never went to Colby," I said. "Doesn't know shit."

CHAPTER
SIX

Guze was a tough kid, a fullback on the football team, with biceps that made his shirt sleeves tight, and the intensity of a wolverine when he got in a fight. We were the only two college kids in the Arena Café, and that made me nervous. If you were drinking with Guze, the odds on winning any fights you got into went up. The bad part was that the odds on getting into a fight went up too. I was uneasy. This was a town bar, full of lumberjacks and mill workers. I was uneasy, too, because we were waiting for two girls.

"They fuck like bunnies," Guze said, "both of them."

I felt the excitement bore into my solar plexus. It mingled with anxiety. The prospect of being with a girl who fucked like a bunny was a little scary, especially since I'd never actually done it at all, exactly. I felt awkward and sweaty. I dragged on my cigarette.

"Where we going to take them," I said.

"We'll take them in the car. You get in the back with the sister, me and the Shark up front."

"The Shark?"

"Yeah, it's her nickname. I don't know why. Maybe sharks are supposed to fuck a lot." Guze shrugged. "Anyway, I haven't seen her sister, but the Shark says she's good-looking and hot."

"Like me," I said. I drank some beer. "You got any safes?"

"Sure." Guze fumbled in his jacket pocket and came out with a handful of Ramses. He skidded one in its small cardboard box across the tabletop. I picked it up quickly and put it into my shirt pocket.

"You always have a supply handy, Guze?"

"Bet your ass," he grinned. "Big G man from the west, Boonie." He looked across the room. "Here they are."

I wished I hadn't come. I looked at the two girls as they slid into the booth with us. One beside Guze, the other one beside me. The one with Guze looked a little like a shark: dark and smooth and not exactly sharp-featured but sort of a streamlined face. Her hair was black and cut short and brushed back like Doris Day wore hers, with a pompadour in the front.

"Boonie, this is Shark."

I said hi.

"Hi, Boonie, this is my sister, Barb."

"Hi, Barb, how ya doing?"

"Nice to meet you."

Barb was smaller than Shark and younger. It was hard to tell. Maybe she was pretty young. But she had tits; you could see them. She had slid her coat back off her shoulders and her sweater was tight. Her hair was lighter than her sister's and she wore it shoulder length. Her face was like Shark's but less complete, more tentative. She had on very red lipstick. Her nails were short, as if she bit them.

I said, "Want a cigarette?"

Barb said, "Sure."

I shook one out of my pack of Camels and she took it. I lit a match, cupping it inside one hand, and lit her cigarette. She held it out near the tips of her fingers and I don't think she inhaled. I was in a panic. I couldn't think of anything to say.

"So where you from?" Barb said, moving her cigarette in front of her face, waving the smoke away.

"New Bedford, Mass.," I said.

"That's a long ways."

"It's not a long way," I said. "This is a long way."

"Huh?"

"You go to school?" I said.

"Sure," she said. She puffed on her cigarette.

A big waitress shuffled over. Her arms, in her short-sleeved dress, were fat and solid looking. She wore old fleece-lined bedroom slippers.

"Four beers," Guze said, making a circular gesture with his right hand. The waitress shook her head.

"They won't bother us about under-age college kids," she said, "but not the girls." She looked at Barb. "How old are you, honey? For crissake, you're about fifteen."

"I'm twenty-one," Barb said, and puffed on her cigarette.

The thick-bodied men at the next table were looking at us. I felt kiddish and ineffectual. Barb's face was a little flushed. The waitress grunted.

"You can't stay in here," the waitress said. "You're too young."

Guze took a five-dollar bill out of his pocket and folded it in half, the long way, and showed it to the waitress.

"You're sure you don't want to change your mind?" he said.

The waitress gestured with her thumb toward the door. "Beat it," she said.

I didn't want to be the first to get up, although all of me trembled to leave. "Why don't we pick up some booze and take a ride," I said. Inside my voice sounded small and piping, like a child's. Guze nodded.

"Yeah, this place sucks anyway," he said. He dropped the five on the table and walked toward the door without looking back. We followed him, the two girls, and me last. I slowed, frightened, by the table full of men, so it wouldn't look as if I were running. None of the men looked up, and I swaggered slightly, keeping myself between the girls and the men, as we left the bar. Outside I felt relief and self-satisfaction. I had been brave walking past the men; they'd had plenty of chance to give me lip and they hadn't. Now if this little babe would let me fuck her . . .

It was mid-November in central Maine, but the weather was warm. It had been cold the previous week, but the way it did sometimes, it had warmed, and you could walk around in a Windbreaker. It seemed like early fall as we drove up toward the college in a car Guze had borrowed. We had a pint bottle of Ballantine's scotch that we passed around. It tasted to me at the time like one of those medications taken to induce vomiting. Always in the movies it looked good when the men rode in and bellied up to the bar and poured a big drink. I took a pull at the bottle and passed it to Barb. I gave no sign that it tasted dreadful. Barb drank and gave no sign either. Guze swung the car onto the road behind the dorms and pulled up on the far side of Johnson Pond.

"Shark and I are going to take a walk down by the lake," Guze said. "Keep the bottle."

Then we were alone in the back seat. I drank again from the bottle and forced myself not to shiver. I held it toward Barb.

"Want another shot?" I said.

"Sure," she said. She drank.

Across the pond the lights of the fraternity houses were bright. With the windows down we could hear the sounds of radios and record players and occasional shouts. I took some more scotch. My stomach burned with it.

"You like college?" Barb said.

I said, "Yes," and lunged against her as if I were plunging through a window. She put her mouth against mine and opened it and stuck her tongue out. I felt the hot red surge that I would feel again, a surge that wasted all inhibition, that brooked no hesitance. Barb with her tongue motionless in my mouth went supine on the back seat, face up, with me clumsily on top of her. *Jesus Christ, she's going to let me.* And she did. She lay perfectly still while I fumbled under her blouse and felt her small breasts inside her pointy, wired bra. She lay perfectly still while I put my hand inside her underpants, and perfectly still while I pulled them down over her thighs awkwardly with one hand. Still with one hand I got my fly unzipped, and she lay watching me with a slight quirk of a smile that rested without movement on her mouth. When I got my pants down she reached out and took hold of me the way a child might hold its father's finger. I remember us that way, frozen in time, her face in that fixed small smile, holding on to me, motionless as I looked down at her in the back seat of a 1946 Ford sedan.

I said, "Can you help me put it in?"

She stared up at me and made no sign that she'd heard, but she let go of me and put her legs apart and I managed on my own.

When it was over she put her underpants back on. In the bright moonlight they were white cotton, puckered at the waistband from laundering. We sat silently and drank some more scotch until Guze and Shark came back and we drove the girls back downtown.

CHAPTER
SEVEN

Guze and Billy Murphy and I were kneeling in a rear pew in Our Lady of the Immaculate Conception Church at 7:20 on a Saturday night. There were short lines at each confessional.

"The French priest is in the booth on the left," Billy whispered. "He can't understand English. He just gives you three Our Fathers and three Hail Marys no matter what you tell him."

"You never had nothing to tell him, Billy," Guze said.

The smell of candle wax lingered in the chill silence of the church. An elderly man and woman knelt before us, saying penance. I wondered what they had left to confess.

"What if he's not in that booth," I said. "The other guy is brutal."

A young woman with a kerchief over her head walked up from the altar. Her heels clicked in the silent church. Her hands were clasped in front of her. She looked down at them as she walked. On either side of the altar there were banks of candles flickering in red jars. Above the altar arch the Lamb of God looked sweetly down and cherubim were poised in holy ecstasy along the rim of the arch. I could feel the infinite reach of sanctity stretching back along hushed passages of time, in living connection with Dickensian England and the France of Charlemagne, with Bethlehem and Eden. Church had surely felt this way to Shakespeare, to Columbus, to Niccolo Machiavelli; clear and cool and breathless with the memory of ancient sacrifice; the sloe-eyed virgin holding her child; the sacred heart, crimson in the middle of the martyred breast; frozen in statuary that seemed coeval with the events memorialized.

It was my turn in the booth. Kneeling in the confessional, I murmured the familiar formula, my throat narrow with embarrassment. "Bless me, Father, for I have sinned. My last confession was a month ago and these are my sins." There was a small velvet drape across the window between me and my confessor, and I could only sense the presence on the other side as it shifted slightly, and its breath whistled faintly in its nose. ". . . and I had intercourse."

"How many times?"

"Once, Father."

"Say t'ree Hail Mary and t'ree Our Father and make good act of contrition," the presence said, and began to murmur in Latin the prayer I said in English. Our lowered voices murmured in unison. He finished before I did. Priests always did. I took my time on the prayer so I wouldn't seem to take it lightly. Then it was over and I

was in a pew kneeling to say my penance, relief tingling
along the edges of my body. My hands were damp. But I
was safe. *I dread the loss of heaven and the pains of hell.*
How could those few red rushing moments be worth an
eternity of damnation? What a fool I had been, and yet,
in the whispering cool church with its flickering candles
burning for the dead, I knew that I would do it again. I
knew that if I got the chance, that rage would sweep
over me and I would plunge ahead though the pit gaped
sulphurously beneath us. I tried to think of God, of the
Virgin. The feeling kept its claim on my soul even as I
prayed. Could I be forgiven for something I knew I'd do
again? Jennifer. I'd like her to know I wasn't a virgin
anymore. I wished I knew her well enough to tell her.
She'd look at me so interested, so fully concentrated on
what I was saying, and I knew she'd think it was good. It
wasn't just the fooling, it was the pleasure of being one of
those who had and I knew she'd think that was nice and
she'd laugh when I told her about it and color the way
she did when she laughed.

The vaulted ceiling of the church darkened toward
the peak and you couldn't see where the arching rafters
met beneath them. I still knelt alone in the pew toward
the front of the church and smiled. Jennifer would like it.
I couldn't wait to tell her, if only I knew her better.

She'd laugh about hell. I knew she wasn't Catholic.
I'd barely talked to her, yet I paid such close attention to
her, to everything she said and did in my presence, to everything I heard, to everything I imagined about her,
that I felt sure of her as if I knew her best of all. I knew
knew she'd be delighted.
she wouldn't disapprove of me screwing some townie. I

And I thought about her in the limpid stillness of the
dim church while I knelt, and I thought of Barb on her
back with her legs apart and as I felt the surge of desire
in my belly, I tried to think of the Virgin. For a moment
Jennifer and Barb and the Holy Mother all blended in
my imagination and for a moment my passion was multi-
ple and two-thirds holy.

Oh my God, I said, *Oh dear God make her love me.*
Then I stood and walked, trembly and thick with passion,
from the silent church.

CHAPTER
EIGHT

The library reading room, deal tables, bright lights, maps and reference books, the low buzz of talk, sharp outbursts of male laughter and female squeal. "Nick said you could help me with *Hamlet*, Boonie," Jennifer said. Black sweater, simple string of pearls. "My professor said Hamlet's tragic flaw was original sin." Her breath smelled of cigarette smoke, her hair of perfume as she bent toward me.

"Sure, sit down." The rustle of her wide gray skirt. Her elbow touched me. More perfume. Her knee touched mine briefly. "He means sort of nobody's perfect," I said. "He means that because the world's not perfect you can't control it and the best anybody can do is be ready, you know?"

Cigarette smoke on her breath again and hint of Colgate, her mouth wide and smiling, her eyes the shape of almonds but much larger. "What in hell has that got to do with original sin?"

I leaned back a little in my chair. Expansive. "I

didn't say it was a swell answer, your professor is kind of vague, but you know the theory of original sin?"

Her smile again and the laugh lines deepening around her mouth; a tiny shadow formed beneath her lower lip when she smiled. "I believe it involves fucking," she said. And both of us burst into laughter in the quiet hall.

Jennifer never drank much beer. Everyone said she did, but she didn't. "I hate it," she told me. "Never tell, because if you're going to date, you have to drink beer. Nobody drinks anything else."

"Except in hotels they don't serve anything else in this state." She hadn't known that. She didn't know a million things. I drank my beer and got two more. Hers was half finished. I drank it. I didn't care if she knew anything or everything, but it was hard to figure how someone so wonderful could know so little. She didn't know where Omaha was. She didn't know that Benny Goodman had given a concert in Carnegie Hall in 1938. She cared nothing about the Brooklyn Dodgers. She'd never seen a play. Her feet on the seat under her, ballerina slippers. A white blazer.

"Why do you know so much, Boonie?" Her nails were glossy and slightly pointed. Her hands looked strong. A red pack of Pall Malls, Teresa Brewer on the jukebox, smoke and maybe the faint smell of clean sweat in the crowded bar.

"I don't know," I said. "I guess it must be I'm very smart."

Her eyes were blue. Jennifer said, "Maybe it's not such an asset. Maybe it's better to know what you need to."

"Once more," Olivier said, "into the breech, dear friends." The theater half empty, Jennifer and I had our feet dangled over the backs of the chairs in front of us. Jujyfruits, Black Crows, the smell of popcorn, the smell of damp woolen coats, darkness, and the ray of projected light from the back to the screen.

"They're not talking Shakespeare," Jennifer whispered. Her lipstick smelled a little like raspberry Jell-O as she leaned toward me to whisper.

"Yes, they are," I said. "They're just saying it right."

Snow from our boots melted in small puddles under the seats. We sat together without touching.

At the door of her dormitory at ten o'clock she was kissing Nick good night. The collar of her camel's-hair coat was up, she was on her toes, white socks, penny loafers, her face up toward Nick. Me she could have kissed flatfooted. Nick's left hand was on her backside. There was some snow, not heavy, big flakes, drifting in the lights in front of the dorms. I said good night to my date, who seemed in a hurry to go in. Jennifer stopped kissing Nick and turned her head against his chest and saw me. She winked. I took Nick's hand and moved it up to the small of her back. "I don't want you getting more than I did," I said.

"Nobody could get less, Boonie," Nick said. We

laughed. Walking away from them I felt short of breath
and my eyes stung in the crystal-flaked darkness.

We were in a booth in the spa; most people were in
class and it was quiet in the spa. Jennifer gave me one of
her Pall Malls. Each of us sat sideways on our side of the
booth, feet out along the rest of the booth seat. Jennifer
had on saddle shoes. "What's a cockteaser, Boonie?" Her
face was somewhat oval. On one cheek was an almost im-
perceptible scar. Scraped it as a small child, she'd told
me. I was the only one, she said, who'd ever noticed it.

"A cockteaser is a girl who makes you think she'll
come across and doesn't," I said.

Her face was serious. She nodded. "I figured something like that because of the *teaser* part. But what's a
cock?"

I grinned. "Jesus Christ," I said, "doesn't Marblehead
have a bad element? Didn't they teach you anything?"

I was thrilled to explain things to her. There was so
much she didn't know. I could tell her things forever.

"No, no, no," she said with that thrilling lilt in her
voice that she had, "no making fun. If I can't ask you,
Boonie, who can I ask?" Her face was serious now. "Everyone else I have to pretend with."

I wasn't sure I could talk; my throat was constricted.
It was hard to swallow. As I breathed I felt as if my
breath trembled in and out. "A cock is another name for a
penis. Originally it meant a spigot, or faucet, and by, you
know, analogy, it became slang for the other thing."

She seemed pleased to know that. She made me feel

I'd pleased her. It was years before I understood that she
made everyone feel that way.

In a skin-tight one-piece black Lastex bathing suit a
girl named Fritzi swam slowly past the dock in an expert
Australian crawl, her long white arms stretching out
fully, her breast arching out of the water with each
reaching stroke. Six or eight of us watched her. Keg beer
in big paper cups, chino pants, white shirts with button-
down collars, the cuffs turned up, somebody's camp at
the lake, I never knew whose. Among the trees charcoal
smoke and the smell of grilling meat. Feeny the Nar-
ragansett beer salesman used to get us the keg and tap it
for us. He often stayed at the party, only a couple years
out of college, not much older than we were, stocky and
full of laughter. The beer came mostly foam at first until
it settled down from the trip out from town. I had to
keep the paper cup tilted so the beer slid down the side
and even then it took a while to fill.

"Want to take a walk, Boonie?" Jennifer was wearing
gray flannel Bermuda shorts and a man's white shirt with
the tails tied in front. Her thick white socks were halfway
up her tan calves. I handed her the beer I had drawn and
took another cup and got a second one full. I didn't want
to make her wait, so it was mostly foam. Didn't matter. I
could come back. It was still May and the summer homes
around the lake were empty. We walked on the thick
pine carpet under the high-branched long-bodied white
pines. Pines high enough and thick enough to have
suppressed the underbrush. It was mostly clear going on
the thick needle carpet.

"Where's Nick?" I said.

She sipped a little of the beer from the big cup. A wisp of foam stayed on the bridge of her nose when she lowered the cup. I reached over and wiped it away.

"He went to Bowdoin this weekend," Jennifer said. "I came with Bruce Walter." Behind us the sounds of the party were clear. Laughter in two octaves, the sound of splashing as people dove into the lake; somebody honked the horn on their car in shave-and-a-haircut-two-bits rhythm.

Jennifer said, "I think there's something wrong with him." Her lipstick looked slightly smudged and her mouth had that slightly red look around it that it always got when she'd been doing a lot of kissing.

"Bruce? Why do you think there's something wrong with him?" I wasn't drunk yet, but I would be in a while.

"He's so aggressive," she said. "It's not natural. He's grabbing and, you know, shunting and . . . he tried to put my hand on it and he's . . ." She shook her head. "He's sick."

There was a tree down and we leaned our backs against it and drank our beer. The lake glistened through the trees. The sounds of the party off to our left. In the trees around us the movement of squirrels and birds. "My love," I said, "Bruce isn't sick, he's horny. He's normal. All guys are like that. Some of them just inhibit it more, you know?" We were side by side against the tree, our feet pointed out before us, Jennifer's loafers exactly side by side, toes straight.

"I know, I mean I expect guys to try. I don't blame them for trying, but he's so . . . so persistent and he gets so excited. In him it's not affection. It's his needs and it doesn't take account of what I want." Jennifer didn't know the dates of the Civil War. But she knew what she needed to know. Maybe better than I did.

"You want to stay with me?" I said. She nodded.

I worked that summer loading trucks in a Coca-Cola plant out on Kempton Street in New Bedford. Every day from ten in the morning till seven at night I took cases off the roller track and heaved them into a truck. The top of the truck always had broken glass on it and when you loaded tops and shoved the cases across you usually scraped your forearms. I had cuts on both arms all summer. One weekend I borrowed a car and went up to Marblehead and visited Jennifer. Sarah Vaughan was singing at a club in Magnolia and we went down in the warm evening, just she and I. Her friend couldn't go and it was almost like a date. I had on my summer dress-up white linen jacket, white oxford-weave shirt, button-down collar, black knit tie, gray slacks, loafers, no socks. Jennifer had on a full skirt and a peasant blouse. She sat easily and poised in the front seat with me and talked as we drove north through Salem and Beverly. Settling darkness, people still out, a lot of them on front steps, the radio on. Vaughn Monroe, "Dance Ballerina Dance," Larry Clinton, Bea Wain, "Deep purple falls over sleepy garden walls." "She's married to André Baruch," I said. Jennifer was never aware peripherally. Her alertness was always concentrated on one thing. "Bea Wain," I said. "The girl singing. She's married to an announcer named André Baruch who sounds sort of like Basil Rathbone and did play-by-play on the Dodgers for a little while." Jennifer smiled. It was as if I'd explained $E=mc^2$. The road curved, nearly empty, along the seacoast and the summer trees were deep green and placid.

CHAPTER
NINE

Jennifer said she loved Nick. She loved everyone she went steady with.

"That's not love," I would say, "that's convenience. You can't be in love with two or three people a year."

And she would smile that aching smile and say I could love my way and she could love her way. "What fun would it be," she would say, "to go out with someone without being in love?"

"You got it backwards," I would say, and she would nod and think on it, but I always had a sense that she wouldn't be different because I said she should be.

I was in Onie's with Billy Murphy and Guze drinking beer on a December night when she called me.

"Come and get me," she said. "I need you to come and get me."

"Where?"

"Student Union."

"I'll be up."

I borrowed Dave Herman's Chrysler convertible and

drove up rubbing the frost off the inside of the wind-shield until the heater took hold. Electricity buzzed in the pit of my stomach. *Come and get me,* she had said. *I need you to come and get me.* I was half drunk and tense with excitement and frightened. Both hands on the wheel, I took in a big lungful of smoke without taking the cigarette from my mouth. Nineteen years old, I felt that something was about to happen, something that would fix me forever like an insect caught in amber, something that would commit me beyond deviation or retraction or even regret. God was about to put his mark on me and I knew it and it scared hell out of me. Now, looking back with the forgiving, solicitous, but lordly wisdom of adulthood, I have no quarrel with what I felt then. I was right.

She was sitting alone in the empty Student Union in a big leather armchair near the console radio that stood at the far end of the lounge. It was 8:30 on a Saturday night. But that made no difference. The Student Union was always empty. Rugs, upholstered furniture, piano, card tables, magazines, space, always empty, just like the lounges in Boys' Clubs and YMCAs. Later I would see similar lounges in USOs and military day rooms, always empty, and in their emptiness, a symbol of the echoing void between the young and those who administered them.

She had on a black cashmere cardigan sweater and a plaid skirt. She got right up when she saw me.

"I got my white charger outside," I said. "Want to get up behind and ride off?"

"Yes."

"Where you want to go?"

"I don't care. I just had to get away from Nick."

I held her camel's-hair coat and she slipped into it and I smelled her perfume, and barely, beneath the musk, the scent of her, which was a little like the scent of crushed bittersweet leaves that my father had taught me to chew when I was very small.

In Herman's Chrysler again we drove slowly downtown.

"Nick wanted to get engaged," Jennifer said.

"And you didn't want to?"

"No."

"Probably thought you loved him," I said.

"Well, I . . ." She stopped and looked over at me. I couldn't see her face in the dark car, but I felt bad. It was an easy point and she didn't need to be scored on right now.

"What I felt was affection—what he wants is ownership," she said.

"Sometimes," I said, "it almost seems that you're even smarter than I am."

She smiled at me.

I could feel the tension shivering along my arms. I felt as if I were trembling internally.

"Want to go to Bill's Café?" I said. "No one ever goes there. We'll be alone."

She nodded. I thought about Nick at the frat party looking for his date, full of himself and his surprise, the ring in his pocket, looking for Jennifer and slowly realizing something and feeling the sickness in his stomach and the humiliation and feeling alone.

Bill's served draft beer in steins for thirty cents. We each had one. Across from me Jennifer's face was almost gaudy with possibility, serious and grateful, full of relief, intensely interested in me, affectionate, gorgeous, and electric with personality, dense with contained animation, beautiful beyond correlative, desirable beyond speech. I was numb with desire, terrified with epiphany, barely able to breathe.

"I'm sorry to break up your Saturday night, Boonie," she said.

My throat was nearly closed. I took a shallow breath and said, "You didn't." My voice was hoarse, I could hear it shaking. "I would rather be with you than do anything else on earth."

She smiled and looked down and took a tiny swallow of her beer. I struggled for steadiness. Here it was, my life, every happiness, all meaning, here staring at me, now, not yet twenty years old and I had to turn the corner and win it or lose it right now, without help, with almost no experience, with my emotions tearing about inside in jagged and mongrel confusion.

I said, "You got to tell him."

Jennifer's head came up and she stared at me. "Nick?" she said.

"Yes. You can't just walk off and leave him like that."

"Oh, I'll talk with him tomorrow," Jennifer said. She smiled her thrilling smile.

"But he loves you," I said. I felt as if I were shivering visibly, but my hands on the table seemed still.

Jennifer stared at me again. Her face was too rich, too interesting ever to look blank. But there was in the vibrant complexity of her look the trace of incomprehension. "Well," she said, "he'll stop."

"Call him up," I said. "You have to tell him. Have

him come down. I'll stay with you. Do you want to go out with me tomorrow?"

She nodded.

"And Monday?"

She nodded.

"The rest of the week?"

"Yes," she said. "I'd like to a lot."

Steadiness surged through me, it suffused me, it warmed and solidified my soul and all things were possible and nothing was fearsome.

"Call Nick, tell him you're with me, and tell him to come down and talk. When he gets here, tell him it's over. Tell him you've decided to go with me, or whatever is the truth. You owe him the truth."

"Boonie," she said. "Why? Why do that? Why hurt him?"

"The other way would hurt him more," I said. "And it would hurt you."

"How would it hurt me?"

"It's not honorable," I said. She had to be honorable. She had to be everything. She was my future. She had to live up to that, to my standards.

"He's so big," Jennifer said, looking at me. "What if he has a fit or something?"

"He's bigger than I am, but I'm much quicker," I said. "Call him. It'll be all right."

And it was. It was more than all right. It was touching and sad and dignified and full of nobility in a way that only the affairs of children can be. Nick came down and he and Jennifer talked at the table while I leaned on the bar out of earshot and drank my beer. When it was over Nick came over to the bar with Jennifer. He put out his big hand and we shook. "Take care of her," he said. I nodded. He turned and walked out of the bar. Jennifer and I looked at each other.

"You're right," she said. "It was better this way." But there was a very small line between her eyebrows as if she were frowning to herself. When I drove her back to her dorm we were quiet and when I dropped her off I was scrupulous not to touch her. No good-night kisses, no hugs. There was no large plan at work. I was simply scared to. I had little reason as yet to think women cherished my affection, and I didn't want to force it on Jennifer.

"I'll pick you up at seven tomorrow?" I said.

"Oh, Boonie, I'd love it if you would," she said. And smiled at me. And went into the dorm. It was cold, three weeks before Christmas; the high, clear stars must have looked this way two thousand years ago.

I drove Herman's car back to the ATO house and found him and Guze and Billy Murphy in the living room drinking Ballantine's scotch from the bottle. I joined them. The bottle passing from one to the next, and each of us ritually wiping the bottle mouth. I drank without speaking my secret until I was calm enough to sleep.

CHAPTER
TEN

Driving Dave Herman's car up from town I said, "We've been out every night this week and we haven't even made out."

"I know," Jennifer said.

"One of those nights I may hook a left up here at Johnson Pond and be all over you," I said. "So be alert."

At the fork I bore right.

Jennifer said, "Chicken," her voice low and full of implication.

I U-turned the old Chrysler and headed out behind Johnson Pond, where freshman year I had scored my only point with the Shark's kid sister. It was early Friday night. No one else was parked there. The lights swept out across the frozen pond as I turned in and stopped. I shut off the lights but left the engine running. The heater was on high.

I half-turned and looked at her. She was sitting neither next to me nor against the door. The light from the college across the pond made it easy to see in the car. Her oval face was white and her mouth was dark against it. Only her eyes were invisible, dark shadows in her face. The radio played Jimmy Ricks, who used to be the lead singer with the Ravens. He sang "Love Is the Thing" in his bottomless bass voice. Jennifer turned her head and looked at me with her smile and her eyes shadowed. She wore a navy peajacket with collar up and with her dark hair she seemed almost a disembodied face pale and magical in the car. The moment was crystalline, and careful, and unhurried. I put my arm out to her and she slid toward me on the seat and shifted easily so that her face turned up. I closed my arms around her and kissed her and felt my soul go out of me and suffuse us. We kissed for a long time and when we stopped there were tears stinging my eyes wonderfully. She leaned her head against me, looking up, and now I could see her eyes, and a look that I can only call enchantment was in them.

"I love you," I whispered.

She nodded her head against my shoulder.

"Do you love me?" I said.

She nodded again.

"Say it," I said.

"I love you," she said.

"Not right now, I know we're too young, but later, when we graduate, will you marry me?"

She moved her head against my shoulder again.

"Will you?"

Her head nodded.

"Say it."

"I'll marry you," she said. Her voice was small.

The wind skittered swirls of light snow across the frozen pond so that it looked dusty. We sat perfectly silent listening to the radio, looking out across the pond. I had my arms around her. She had her face pressed against my chest. I was complete. Reunified. Whole.

"I will be special," I said. "I will be somebody. I will take you where other people couldn't. I know it sounds braggy and like teenage crap, but I am not like everyone else. I will be special for you."

She didn't say anything but shifted slightly and leaned a little harder against me. I felt a kind of vertigo, as my self spiraled down into oblivion, fusing with her and becoming us. I was gone. Even now, looking back from so long a distance, the years before Jennifer, when I was merely I, seem unimaginable, as unreal as baby pictures—the blank, roundfaced infant that is only technically me.

"Shall we get married right after graduation?" I said.

"Maybe."

"We could get married sooner and live in the vets' apartments."

"What would we do for money?"

I put my face against the top of her head. "Money will come," I said. "You can always get money."

"How?"

"I could work."

"What about school?"

"We could quit," I said.

She was quiet and I had a sense that I was going too fast, that she was maybe a little breathless. A week ago she was dating Nick Taylor. Now I was speaking of quitting school and getting married.

"Or we could wait till graduation," I said.

"Yes," she said. Her voice was muffled against my chest.

CHAPTER
ELEVEN

We were together almost all the time. When we parted at night I sometimes stood on the sill of her first-floor window and talked with her until the campus police chased me away . . . between classes we drank coffee together in the spa . . . after class we went to the library, or sat in her dorm living room and read aloud to each other, homework, newspapers, popular novels. Evenings there were parties with kegs of beer and three-piece bands, chaperons ill-at-ease, caught between embarrassment and the demands of the college, kissing and the press of bodies, boisterous affection among the men cloaked by insult, and always I moved in the miasma of her splendor, contained in her radiant presence like a saint in a halo. To everyone but me the romance was sudden. One week and we spoke of marriage. I knew it wasn't sudden and perhaps she did, too, knew it in the inarticulate way she knew things, knew it without knowing it, in the way she had of ignoring what didn't apply at the moment. I had loved her since I saw her. Loved her, or the imagined her, before I'd met her. Loved her before I was able to understand what love meant, before I knew of sex, loved her since I could feel and had spent my life waiting to meet her and then waiting to have her love me.

Her mother's couch was rough tweed and made friction burns on exposed skin as we struggled joyfully on it.

"Would you take off your clothes?"

"Take them off for me."

She lay still as I unbuttoned her cashmere sweater and slipped it back over her unresisting shoulders and pulled her arms from the sleeves. Her skirt zipped at the side and I unzipped it and edged it down her thighs. She arched her body compliantly and lifted her butt at the right time. She wore a white bra and white nylon underpants. She raised up slightly so I could unhook the bra. "It has little hooks," she murmured. I undid the hooks and she put her arms up so I could slide the bra off forward. The lights were out in the living room but the streetlight spilled through the front window and everything was clear and bright. She lay back and raised her pelvis again and I slipped the nylon underpants down along her thighs and off. She lay back perfectly still and smiled at me. I'd never seen a live woman naked before. Shark's sister, Barb, had been up-with-the-dress-in-with-the-member. I stood and looked at her. She didn't seem embarrassed. She seemed tranquil. I took off my own clothes and lay back down beside her on the couch. She opened her arm for me and I pressed against her in the curve of it. I kissed her; she opened her mouth. I touched her. I ran my hands over her. She touched me. The passion rushed through me; I hugged her to me in thundering darkness. Both of us were damp with sweat. She put her hands on either side of my face and raised my face from hers.

"We shouldn't," she said.

"I know," I said.

"I might get pregnant."

Our voices were hoarse.

"It would spoil it for the honeymoon," I said. "For us it wouldn't be right." We pressed still hard against one another.

"I wouldn't trust a safe," she said.

Shivering with the effort I lay still beside her. "We'll wait," I said. "When we get married I want it all just right."

The sun was bright and the snow, four feet deep over most of the campus, was beginning to melt. The runoff, channeled through the shoveled paths, turned the bare ground to mud. I held Jennifer's hand as we squished through the mud toward her dorm.

"I wouldn't want my children brought up Catholic," Jennifer said. I felt the flutter of fear in my chest.

Before I spoke again I knew that my religion had ended. It was as simple as that, and I was startled by it. It conflicted with Jennifer and so it was gone. Twenty years of often impassioned belief, of dark confessionals and cool churches, of Latin prayers and Gregorian chants, of complexity, and mystery, and time, washed away in casual conversation in a muddy Maine spring.

"I'm not really Catholic anymore," I said.

The ocean rolled in among the rocks at Christmas Cove. The sun baked the rocks hot and the spray cooled them. In small depressions among the rocks were tiny pools; the remnants of high tide lay still and warm. Jennifer dipped a naked big toe in one and stirred it absently. Her toenails were painted red. "Why are you so mad," she said.

I squatted beside her in a bathing suit and T-shirt. My nose was peeling. "We love each other," I said. "We are supposed to stay together."

Jennifer's bathing suit was blue and strapless with white piping. "Oh, come on, Boonie," she said. "You were having a nice time over there, and I couldn't stand Billy's date so I went over with Bobbi and John and those people. It's not like I ran off with someone."

I still squatted, shaking my head a little. "Then tell me and I'll go with you, but don't leave me. We're supposed to be together."

Jennifer's face showed that hint of fine puzzlement that I'd seen before. "But Billy's your friend. I didn't want to hurt his feelings."

I sat down on the rough rock beside her and put my arms around her and pulled her against me and we went over and lay on our sides, facing. "Doesn't matter, friends, hurt, not hurt, mother, father, anything. Only you and I matter. You have to understand that. Only you and I. Nothing else. Nothing." And I kissed her and she kissed me back in the baking sun at the edge of the Atlantic.

The letter was on Colby stationery, Office of the Dean. It said: "Dear Mr. Adams, I regret to inform you that your academic record is unsatisfactory. Your personal conduct has been disruptive, and thus can hardly mitigate in your favor. I am therefore compelled to inform you that we cannot accept you as a student here at Colby for the fall semester. If you have questions about this decision, or need help in pursuing a course of study and conduct whereby you might be reconsidered in the spring semester, please call my secretary, or come to my office and make an appointment to see me. I regret this decision, as you must, but your scholarship and citizenship, or more accurately lack of both, leave me no other choice. Sincerely, Casper A. Brady, Dean." . . . They drafted me in August.

The bus took ten hours to go from the Boston army base to Fort Dix Induction Center. We got to bed at 3:45 and were up at five standing, still in civilian clothes, in ragged rank in the company street. . . . Each time the M1 fired, its recoil jammed my right thumb against my right cheekbone. After three days on the range the cheek was puffy and sore with a faint purple tinge to it. "Lock and load," one of the range cadre yelled. "One round ball ammunition." We were sprawled in the prone position on the cold gravel. Next to me a kid from Brooklyn named Garfi murmured, "Lock and load your fucking ass." I fired on command and the thumb banged against my puffy cheek and the bright brass casings looped sequentially out to the right.

Long, partitioned desks painted OD, the burble of dits and dahs in my earphones meant nothing. "Use some word tricks, asshole," the instructor said. "What's S sound like?" All fifty of us responded in derisive, bored, and hostile unison. "Chickenshit, sir." With his hands on his

hips and his fatigues starched and his blue combat infan-
tryman's badge pinned over his pocket, the instructor
said, "Right, assholes. You better fucking remember it
when you go to frozen Chosan, 'cause it's two-thirds of
SOS. What's Q sound like?" Again the unison response.
"Here comes the bride." The instructor smiled widely.
"Very good, fuckballs, listen to it." He pressed his key
and the sound came through my earphones, dah, dah, dit,
dah.

We sat together on her mother's couch. I had a diamond ring in my pocket. "I'm going to Fort Lewis, Washington," I said, "to a repple-depple."

Jennifer's head was on my shoulder. "A what?"

I squeezed her. "All us GIs talk that way. A replace-
ment depot. Means I'm going to the Far East."

Outside, the late fall rain rushed down and the wind
that was with it made the bare tree branches toss. The
streetlight that lit the room threw heaving shadows
across it.

"Does that mean Korea?"

I shrugged, struggling to be manly. "Probably, that's
where the war is. But it could be Japan, or Okinawa."

Jennifer's voice was small. "I don't want you to go."

I didn't say anything. The shadows tossed about the
room and the rain sheeted against the windows.

"I know you don't want to get married till I come
back," I said. I could barely talk. It would be a year or
more without her. If I didn't get killed. I wouldn't get
killed. "But"—I took the ring out of my pocket—"how
about you wear this while I'm gone?"

She looked at the ring that I held out and didn't take it. She said, "Oh, Boonie."

I held it out in front of her. She stared.

"You're not going to call up Nick Taylor and ask him to come get you, are you?" I said.

Her face shifted from the ring to me. It was more serious than I'd ever seen it.

"Try it on," I said.

She did, slowly, and then held it out and admired it on her hand. "Oh, Boonie," she said. The ring was too big, but I knew it could be fixed. It had belonged to my grandmother.

"We can have it reset if you want."

She looked at the ring and again at me. "Boonie," she said, "I can't."

Outside, the wind drove the rain persistently against the windows. From the kitchen I heard the refrigerator cycle on. "Do you love me?" I said.

She nodded. "Yes. But you have to trust that, just trust it without trying to tie me to you."

In the far corner of the living room was a baby grand piano. Jennifer's high school graduation picture stood on it in a gold-trimmed leather frame. Very glamorous, long hair, head tilted back, gazing upward in profile. The clock on the mantel said ten of nine. But it wasn't. The clock wasn't wound. It always said ten of nine.

"Will you marry me when I come back?" I said.

"I will love you while you're gone, and love you when you come back," she said.

I put out my hand and she took off the ring and put it on my upturned palm. I folded my hand slowly over it and put the ring in my pocket. My eyes burned.

"I gotta walk," I said.

"I'll go with you," she said.

We put on raincoats and she put a kerchief over her head and we walked in the rushing downpour for an hour in near perfect silence. The rain on my face helped hide the fact that I was crying. I kissed her good-bye at her door.

"Are you all right?" she said.

"Yes."

"Do you understand?" she said.

"No."

CHAPTER
TWELVE

The troop ship was awash with vomit. It was ankle deep in the heads and it made the ladders slippery and sloshed along the deck. Sometimes I was the only one in the mess hall, eating by myself while even the cooks and servers were sick. Not being sick, I had a lot of time to think. Leaning on the rail, staring at the empty Pacific, at night trying to sleep in the bunks stacked five high in compartments jammed with duffel, working ration-breakdown details in the hold, I thought about Jennifer and about me. There was no mail, of course, and nineteen days across the Pacific I thought about her and feared there'd be no mail when we got to Pusan. There wasn't. But the first letter caught up with me in Pusan, and two more reached me when I was permanently assigned. Things were the same at college. She missed me. She was going to the Bowdoin game that Friday night in Brunswick. She'd write again as soon as she got my new address. And she did. She wrote two or three letters a week, not very long, not very interesting; away from her, unadorned by the

force of her person, her disembodied language tended to
be general and colorless. She'd gotten a B+ in an exam.
The basketball team lost to Bowdoin. Also to Maine. She
saw Guze sometimes, and Billy Murphy. They said hi.
She had a date for the spring dance. No one I knew, a
transfer from Cornell. Nice guy. Didn't mean anything,
just someone to go with. I wrote her every day. We were
working eight on and eight off, on the radios. I wrote
whenever traffic was slow. Letters about how much I
loved her, about what Korea was like, about what a
bunker looked like and what artillery sounded like and
how a communications platoon runs; letters about the
pink-cheeked boy from Wyoming they'd put in charge of
the platoon, letters about what life would be like when I
came home and when we got married and what we'd call
our children, and please don't go out with other people it
depresses me too much. I know we agreed but I can't
stand it, ten thousand miles away, I think about you all
the time. I knew it wouldn't work when I wrote it. I
knew in fact that it would work the wrong way. She'd
continue to go out but she wouldn't tell me anymore. Her
letters made no further mention of dating.

After a few months of eight on and eight off I could
take and receive Morse code at twenty words a minute
while carrying on another conversation. The pink-
cheeked platoon leader came to understand that he knew
nothing about operating a radio and nothing about running wire and calmed down and got out of the way. The
truce came in early summer and my regiment settled in
along the Imjin River. The war ended with me alive. All I
had to do was sweat out the tour and go home. Jennifer
had worked the summer in a resort hotel as a waitress.

Her parents were a little embarrassed, she said, they thought it was quite blue collar, but it got her away from home for the summer and gave her freedom. Sometimes when I wrote her I sent her short stories I'd composed about us, or thinly disguised versions of us. I was always her hero; she was always feminine and yielding, needing me. When I got out I'd be different; I'd learned a lot about what was important and what wasn't. We could live in vets apartments and I could finish school on the G.I. Bill, then I'd write and we could have kids. I thought Michael and Meredith would be good names.

In the middle of her senior year, a month and a half into the Korean winter, Jennifer wrote to say that she and the guy from Cornell had gotten pinned. She knew it would hurt me, and she'd always feel special about me, but she could never quite deal with my intensity, with my totality. She was a little afraid of it. She felt, finally, overpowered, possessed, and she couldn't live like that.

The valves of my life closed like a stone. The beginnings of stillness settled in me. I was inert, limp, without strength; more, it seemed as if I were without structure, as if all tangibility had drained away. I could no longer be upright.

I wrote her a letter back. I begged her. I would always love her, no one could ever cherish her as I would. Wait till I got back, don't do this. It took two weeks for her reply. Meanwhile, I kept writing. All that I was went into the desperate flood of mail. As I wrote the letters my eyes teared, but no one saw me. Her first letter back was balanced and firm. We couldn't change what time had brought about. They were getting engaged at graduation. I was alone in the bunker when I read it; behind me and below, the wide brown river moved slowly. The rest of the landscape was snow-covered and almost treeless. I sank to my knees with the letter in my hand and pressed my face against the sandbag walls of the bunker and never moved when my call letters rattled on the radio. The next day my letters began to come back unopened and the stillness in me spread slowly and numbly over my whole being.

I told no one and each night I sat and wrote her a letter and after they came back unopened for a month, I stopped mailing them. But I wrote them. When they were done I put them in my footlocker with the ones she'd returned. She sent me no more mail.

My unmailed letters to her became a chronicle of my life, and a memorial to her, a manifestation of a truth I'd half-understood in the rainstorm before I left her when we weren't getting engaged. I was trapped. I was simply love's captive and from that time when I'd danced with her at eighteen I would never be free again. No effort of will could ever change that. No one could replace her. No other meaning existed in life. I knew that, as I wrote my unread letters, with a clarity and sureness that time has not modified. Not yet twenty-two, I had loved and lost and my life was without further purpose. And there was so much of it left, a paralyzing long time of it still to go.

CHAPTER
THIRTEEN

The messages came in over the radio in encrypted five-letter groups. They were just sound patterns that translated into nothing. When the message finished I'd send it over to S-2 and never hear of it again. Tony dePietro and I were the best operators in the regiment. We could take code and receive it without even listening, the right hand marking down the meaningless letters as the sounds went from ear to hand without interference from the brain. I liked being good at it. The battalion commander used to brag about us, the regimental hotshots. We were still shorthanded and dePietro and I were still working to voice nets and one CW net alone, taking turns, eight on, eight off. Officers didn't bother us. No one else understood the code and we were in our way indispensable. There was always traffic on the CW net and whenever an officer appeared we'd listen to the traffic, break in with a Q signal to ask if there was any traffic for this station, ask net control to repeat the negative, and generally look busy until the officer left.

"Knowledge is power," dePietro said to me one day

after we'd frightened away an NG captain from S-2 with a blast of Q and Z signals that sounded vital and signified nothing. He was leaving and I was coming on. He hung around and drank coffee with me before he went to sleep.

"New batch of magazines from the Red Cross," de-Pietro said as he finished his coffee. "Movie magazines, *True Romance*. Who the fuck do they think is over here?"

"It's okay," I said. "I got letters to write."

"Your girl?"

"Yeah."

DePietro nodded and picked up his rifle and went out of the bunker. I read the new call letters for my station, checked in with an any-traffic-for-this-station call just to limber up, and settled in to write Jennifer. I did it in a kind of notebook now, a journal, I suppose you could call it, but always I addressed her, and as I wrote I imagined her and felt her presence and the force of her, the richness and energy. Writing her, I could remember what her mouth felt like and what she smelled like.

My Darling Jennifer,

The army is good for keeping you from falling apart. There's enough organization to sort of push all your pieces together. My fatigues are tailored and starched, my pants have a blousing ring and are bloused stylishly low on my shiny combat boots. The boots are jump-laced. My fatigue cap has a fifty-missions crush to it and is kept stiff by soap. I keep my bunk made so tight you can in fact bounce a coin on it (except there aren't any coins, just paper scrip—mpc). When I salute I have a nice honor-guard flourish to it. I can carry a rifle and a prc-10 for 15 miles in full battle dress and swagger when I'm through.

I got the second highest score in the battalion, last week, at the range. If there's a fight at the NCO club, there's twenty guys will jump in on my side. I'm the only guy in the battalion who's been to college and they think I'm a genius (except the officers). I run the radios on auto pilot and think almost not at all. I pay attention to detail. I do what I'm told. I go when they say go and stop when they say stop. I initiate nothing. At night I get drunk. If it weren't for missing you, it's not such a bad life. Time passes and I can walk through it without having to feel anything or decide anything. Good place for a hollow man.

I always signed them, *I love you*, and I put the date at the bottom each day.

I just dated today's when the weather report started coming in from I Corps. They sent it in clear text, which meant I had to pay more attention than usual, but even then so much of it was boiler plate that I could write out the word after I'd heard the first letter most of the time, and I only really had to pay attention to the wind direction and the numbers—velocity, temperature, that stuff.

In a poker game in early March, dePietro won more than the battalion sergeant major had. He traded the IOUs for R&R for him and me. The sergeant major TDY'd two radio operators in from Division and dePietro and I went to Tokyo.

We were taking showers and drinking daiquiris and smoking cigars in a hotel near Shinigawa station, the water cascading over us in hot plenitude. We took turns.

"First shower in a year," dePietro said. "Good as getting laid."

I drank the daiquiri. It had seemed the thing to drink, as unlike military life in Korea as we could think of. The lemon was tart and cold under the deceit of sugar, and both sugar and lemon masked the rum entirely until it settled in my stomach and the warmth spread out. I finished the rest of the glass and took another. There were ten more on the tray.

"Your turn," dePietro said, and stepped out of the shower. I got in. It was the third time. I worked some Prell shampoo into my hair again and rinsed it off, watching the lather plane along my wet body and swirl into the drain. I lathered all over my body again with Lifebuoy soap and scrubbed my nails with a brush, and rinsed again and got out. I looked at dePietro. He shook his head and I shut off the shower. It had been running for more than an hour.

Wearing government issue white boxer shorts with the little tie strings at the side, we sprawled in the western-looking hotel room and finished our daiquiris.

"Tomorrow I'm going to get drunk on wine," dePietro said. "And then I'm going to do maybe bourbon and then vodka and then we'll see how I feel." He started to dress while I finished the last daiquiri. "Want to find some broads?"

I nodded. I put the empty glass back and sat on the bed. Tears began to run down my face. Tony was looking at himself in the mirror and didn't see me. I got up quickly and splashed on cold water and they stopped.

The whorehouse was near the Sugamo train stop. It was probably near the prison, too, but I never saw the prison. The beds were pallets on the floor. The walls were paper and the doors were sliding. There was a deep hot tub in the bathroom and I sat in it with the water to my neck while a smiling Japanese girl with small breasts and not much body hair massaged my neck and shoulders.

"R and R G.I.," she said. "Korea G.I."

"How do you know," I said.

She wrinkled her nose. "Smell," she said, and smiled.

"Jesus Christ," I said, "I took three showers."

She didn't understand. She smiled and shook her head. When we were through she dried me in a large towel and gave me rubber clogs and a kimono and took me back to her room. We lay down on the pallet.

"No suckahatchie girl," she said.

"Okay," I said.

I lay on my back and she sat astride my thighs and rubbed my body. After a while she moved slightly forward and with an economical movement of hands and hips she put me in her and still sitting astride me moved her pelvis cleverly.

Later that night the girls made sukiyaki on a hibachi. DePietro and I drank rice wine with it, the four of us sitting on the floor in the bedroom, the girls serving us pleasantly, saying their few English words and giggling. Almost domestic. The sex and the dining and the foursomeness was a kind hearted and honest imitation, a decent copy of domesticity, an artful and well-intentioned replica of happiness which made my loss more incisive.

It cost 2500 yen.

CHAPTER
FOURTEEN

Jennifer Grayle became Mrs. John Merchent in a gray stone Episcopal church on a small hill in Marblehead in August of 1954. I was there, the recipient of a civilized invitation in formal engraving. Two weeks home from Korea and I wore my white linen jacket and gray slacks and a black knit tie. Only the tie fit, the rest was too big because I was down under 150 pounds, wiry and thin from carrying a radio and a rifle for long distances at a time. The collar of my button-down shirt was about a size big. My belt was pulled three notches tighter and made the tops of my slacks bunch. I still had a G.I. haircut, and looking at my reflection in a car window as I walked toward the church, I thought I looked consumptive. The back of my jacket stood away from my neck.

Jennifer was in white, her bridesmaids in yellow. The groom and his party wore white dinner jackets and black watch cummerbunds. Everything fit them. I was afraid, sitting blankly in the back nearly anesthetized. What if I fainted? What if I went crazy when I saw her?

What if I cried? When she came down the aisle she looked as she always had, tanned, perfectly made up, poised, and full of controlled power. My deep numbness worked. I sat without expression and almost without feeling; the part of me that could feel was already beginning to dwindle, more and more of me was callus tissue. Inside my thickness I watched them meet at the altar, watched them kneel, watched them rise, watched him take the ring from his brother and put it on her finger, watched her brush her veil back, watched them kiss, and watched them walk up the aisle together.

The reception was in a long, rambling, wasp, white country club on the Marblehead-Swampscott line. The orchestra played things like "The Anniversary Waltz," and the leader sang "Because God made thee mine," with his mouth very close to the microphone. There was an open bar. I ordered a shot and a beer. Jennifer stood with her husband in a receiving line. I didn't go near it. I drank my shot and washed it down with beer and ordered another one. Merchent was tall and blond with a golden tan and athletic shoulders. Someone told me he'd been captain of the tennis team at Cornell. He had blue eyes and a cleft in his chin like Cary Grant. The diamond he'd given Jennifer looked like a paperweight. All the guests looked like their clothes had been made in Paris, and all the older women talked with that Northshore honk that distinguished broads whose husbands were successful. I had another shot.

"Friend of the bride?" the bartender said.

"What makes you think so?"

"I work a lot of weddings. Most people drink champagne. A shot and a beer ain't happy drinking."

I didn't answer him, I just held out the empty shot glass. He shrugged and put some blended whiskey in it. The bottle had one of those little chrome spouts in it, and he turned it nicely when the glass was full so none dripped.

There were flowers banked around most of the room —huge arrangements spilling out of big vases, roses, and a bunch of others that I didn't know the names of. The bridesmaids in their yellow and the ushers in their white splashed among the crowd. The bride and groom danced. The son of a bitch danced so well that he was able to make Jennifer look good. I knew she couldn't dance a step. Or she didn't used to be able to. Things change. I leaned my back against the bar. Without looking, I stuck my shot glass back at the bartender. No one else was at the bar. They were all drinking champagne and nibbling canapés from trays that circulated.

"'Nother beer too," I said.

The hot booze was insulating the small feeling part, layering in more protection. I felt full of novocaine. *Here comes the fucking bride*, I murmured to myself. *All dressed in white. Christ, I never even fucked her.* As they danced, Jennifer looked up at her husband. She looked at him just as she had looked at me, and I knew he felt just like I had, that he was all that Jennifer was interested in. She must have looked at Nick Taylor that way. *Poor bastard, no wonder he'd been walking around with a ring in his pocket. Like me. He believed her.* Even drunk I knew it wasn't quite fair to Jennifer. We were talking about different things when we talked about love, my definition didn't have to prevail.

There were tall windows around the open dance

floor. Outside, trees moved in the summer wind and beyond them people played golf on a green rolling course that seemed eternal. The room was air-conditioned and cool, and high-ceilinged. *The rich are different than we are. Yeah, they're cooler.* The colored dresses and the flowers were beginning to blur and the room was starting to look like an impressionist painting. *I better stick to beer. No more shots.* The beer had lost most of its taste. I sipped it from the bottle.

"Boonie, how nice of you to come," Jennifer said. She was in front of me with the groom. He hadn't loosened his tie. His jacket was buttoned. *Neat,* I thought. *The fucking asshole.*

"Thanks for inviting me," I said. I drank some beer.

"Boonie, this is John Merchent. Boone Adams."

He stuck out his clean, strong, tan hand. "Glad to meet you, Boone, I heard a lot about you up at school."

I shook his hand briefly. "Yeah," I said.

"Understand you were in Korea," he said.

"World safe for democracy," I said.

"My roommate at the deke house was in Korea."

"You a deke?"

"Absolutely. I was a deke at Cornell and when I transferred I moved right in. Great house."

"Cornell," I said, "a deke, and a perfect asshole."

"Boonie," Jennifer said.

"Line from *The Naked and the Dead*," I mumbled.

"You're drunk, fella," Merchent said. "Better get yourself under control."

"Whyn't you get me under control, twinkletoes?"

Merchent's brother walked over and two of the

ushers. They all looked like Merchent. Everybody at the wedding looked like Merchent. Except me.

"A whole collection," I said. "A quartet of perfect assholes."

Merchent jerked his head at me and his brother said, "Come on, fella, I think you should leave." He put his hand on my arm. I yanked my arm away.

"Whyn't he throw me out," I said, and lunged at Merchent. He slid me past him almost negligently and his brother and the ushers rushed me out through the hall and into the parking lot. I sprawled on the pavement and scraped my hands.

"Don't come back," Brother said. "We'll have you arrested."

"How 'bout one at a fucking time," I said. I was on my feet, but the parking lot seemed insubstantial. I was having a little trouble standing steady. Brother and the two ushers laughed a little, shook their heads, and walked back into the reception.

I stood alone in the parking lot. The sun was setting. The knee of my pants was ripped. I had gotten blood from my scraped palms on my white jacket. There was nothing to do and nowhere to go. I started walking. Behind me, I heard Jennifer say, "Boonie." I stopped and looked back. She was standing in the door of the club in her wedding dress. "Boonie," she said. "I'm sorry." I nodded and turned back toward the street and kept walking.

She called after me. "Boonie, I know it's corny, but we could be friends." I shook my head and didn't look back.

CHAPTER
FIFTEEN

I arrived in New York wearing jeans, loafers, a blue oxford-weave shirt with a button-down collar, and an army
field jacket with the twenty-fourth division taro leaf
patch on the shoulder. I had no luggage except a gym
bag with the collection of unmailed letters in it that I had
come to call my journal and a couple of new notebooks.
In my wallet was seventeen hundred dollars in muster-
ing-out pay. I was twenty-two.

The one-room apartment I rented on Thompson
Street had been freshly painted. But whoever had done
the painting hadn't scraped the old paint, so the walls
were lumpy. Around the old four-footed tub and pull-
chain toilet, paint had slopped and dried into thick white
scabs. The porcelain surfaces were ineradicably stained,
like the soul of man, and no absolution would ever clean
them. I didn't care.

Dear Jennifer,
    I think about you most of the time. Drinking seems to
help some, but the world seems painfully laughable to

me, and it's hard to concentrate. It's not just that I've lost
you, I've lost me as well. I can't seem to feel that there's
anything important, including myself. Even suicide seems
not worth the effort. I don't especially want to kill myself.
I don't especially want to do anything. That's the real
ball buster. I don't, simply, know what to do. I bought a
typewriter. I suppose I should try to write, but I don't
seem to have anything interesting to say. I've got enough
money for about four more months. According to an ad
I saw in Life *magazine, my life expectancy is 72 years.*
Fifty more to go. It seems long.

I love you

Except for the daily journal entries to Jennifer my
writing didn't happen. I sat every day for a couple of
hours at my kitchen table and looked at the cheap white
paper in the typewriter. But I didn't type anything. I was
spending a lot of money on beer and by December I was
up to 180 pounds, all of it fat, and I was almost out of
money.

I went down to Robert Hall and spent forty-five dollars for a blue blazer and some gray flannel pants. I
bought a tie in Times Square for a buck, then I got the
Times and started reading help wanted ads. Some kind of
writing job, advertising maybe.

It was my twenty-third interview. I'd been doing
about five a day, every day. I didn't have a job, but I was
getting good at interviewing. *No sir, I didn't finish college.*
I felt my military responsibility came first. Yes sir, I know
that advertising's a tough business. The war left me need-
ing action. I couldn't go back to school like a child. Oh

absolutely sir, I've given it a lot of thought. I assessed what I could do that would help me and help my employer. What did I have to market, I asked myself. Writing skills, I decided, and a desire to be where there was action.

I had the patter down quite well now, when I got a chance to use it. Most of the time the interviewer told me about the company and himself and his philosophy of advertising and employment and things.

"Mr. Adams?"

"Yes?"

"Mr. Locke will see you now."

I walked behind the secretary's wiggling buttocks across the big reception area and down the corridor with head-high cubicles on both sides and men in shirt sleeves working at typewriters and into a big private office with a big window that looked out over Madison Avenue and another big window into another big office across the street. There was probably a guy over there having an exit interview. Matter and anti-matter. The secretary smiled and closed the door behind me.

Mr. Locke was sitting with his feet on the window ledge facing out the window, his head tilted back, his eyes closed. He was tall and thin and blond and probably went to Cornell with John Merchent and his ushers. His gray flannel suit jacket hung on a hanger by the door. His blue oxford button-down was open at the neck and his blue and red rep tie was loosened. He wore horn-rimmed glasses and wing-tipped cordovan shoes. The Prince of Madison Avenue. Full uniform.

I stood by his desk. He still sat with his eyes closed.

Maybe I was supposed to launch into my spiel unprovoked. *No sir, I didn't finish college. I felt my military . . . shit.* Locke kept staring at the insides of his eyelids. Then he sat up abruptly, swung his feet down, spun his chair around, and wrote for maybe a minute in longhand on a legal-size pad of blue-lined yellow paper. When he finished he read over what he'd written, made a spelling change, and sat back.

"Hi," he said. "Whitney Locke. I was just writing some poetry."

I nodded.

"You're Boone Adams. Personnel sent you up."

"Yes."

He waved toward a chair. "Sit down, please."

I did. My chair wasn't as nice as his. But I wasn't the copy chief. He sifted through some folders on his desk until he came up with my application and résumé.

"So you want to get into advertising?"

"Yes, sir," I said.

"One of the things I'd suggest right off, and mind you, you want to work in advertising, I can get you in. But first I'd suggest you and the wife get together, maybe go down to the playroom, something like that, get a blackboard and very carefully chart your career plans. Be goal-oriented, think it through, and recognize that no one's going to be giving you any breaks."

"I'm not married, sir."

"That's too bad. It helps if you are. But whatever. Go to that blackboard and make a chart. Where do I want to be in five years? Ten? How long to be copy chief? Will I be satisfied as copy chief?"

I nodded.

He was still looking at my file. "Didn't finish college," he said.

"No, I felt my military responsibility . . ."

"Doesn't matter, it's the wrong college anyway. We only employ men from Princeton or Yale."

"Oh."

He smiled, stood up, and put out his hand. "Good to have talked with you, Boone. Let me know how you make out. Be sure to get that chart worked out and get yourself goal-oriented. Advertising is not a job, it's a career."

We shook hands. I went out.

At the Discretionary Mutual Insurance Company of America they gave me a writing test. In an interview cubicle in the personnel office they put me at a table, gave me a typewriter and a timer, and asked me to write a story based on the proposition that at noontime tomorrow everyone would lose the power of speech. It was my fifty-second job interview. I had twenty minutes. I wrote a thing called "Winterbaum for President" in which an out-of-work Jewish mime of that name found himself suddenly the great communicator in a speechless world, and became president of the U.S.A. Everyone told me it was a really creative piece and they hired me at three hundred and ninety dollars a month to be the editor of their house organ.

My boss was the Manager comma Advertising and Sales Promotion. The comma and the inversion mattered, I discovered. Advertising and Sales Promotion Manager was a lower rank. Only a Manager comma got a chair with arms and a plastic water carafe and a shoulder-high glass-partitioned office. A Director comma got a partition more than head-high and a rug in addition to all the rest. As sales promotion editor I had a desk and a file cabinet and a chair without arms in the pit with all the other groundlings.

"Remember," my boss told me on my first full day, "this magazine is a management tool. It is a sales promotion device, a means of communicating management's point of view to the men in the field."

I nodded. I was sitting in his office in his conference chair. The conference chair had no arms. Directors got conference chairs with arms.

"The field men, the agents are encouraged to view the magazine as theirs, and that's good. It builds a sense of community. But it is not, I say again, *not*, their magazine. It is ours. All copy is approved upstairs by the general sales manager or his designee. Right?"

I said, "Right."

"You're in on the ground floor here, Boone," he said. "You're getting the chance to start a brand-new company pub. You're not taking over something someone else devised. This is new."

"Yes."

"It's a real creative opportunity, and the fact that you proved, with that splendid short story, that you're one hell of a creative guy, you got hired." He laughed. "Winterbaum for President, goddamn. What was that stain he had on his tie?"

"Beet soup," I said.

"Yes. Good job." My boss's name was Walt Waters. He was a tall, crisp, horsey-looking product of Amherst

College and the Discretionary Mutual Executive Training Program.

"Thanks, Mr. Waters," I said.

"Walt, remember, call me Walt. Everyone's first-name here, even Lee."

Lee was the president. When Walt said Lee his voice hushed a bit.

"Okay, Walt."

"Now, let me give you a couple of tips. Being creative isn't enough. You've got to be savvy as well. About the job. About people. About your appearance. Get a sun-lamp, first thing, and keep yourself tanned. Don't overdo it, but a nice understated tan makes a difference."

I nodded.

"And," he said with a swell friendly smile, "get some clothes. Look around. See how some of us are dressed, get the sense of the look, and then go out and open a charge at Brooks Brothers. It's part of the game. Maybe it seems conformist to you. But it makes sense. A good product sells better in a good package. Right?"

"Right."

CHAPTER
SIXTEEN

I was sitting with the general sales manager in Lee's office. Lee, being president, had an office with walls and a ceiling. He had a secretary with a good-looking ass, and he had a mahogany desk as big as a manager comma's office. He looked kind of small sitting behind it, sort of like a white-haired cherub with bright pink cheeks. Probably too long under the sunlamp. Lee was looking at the current issue of *Discretionary Pulse,* the twelve-page four-color sales promotion toilet paper that I wrote and edited once a month. He was not pleased.

"Pat," he said. "You sign off on this magazine every month. Am I right or wrong?"

There was a faint gloss of sweat on the upper lip of the general sales manager. He looked like he needed to urinate. If Lee turned up the volume a little, I thought he might, right through the fabric. Did the Brooks Brothers guarantee cover urine stains? *Now, for Busy Executives, Our New Fearproof Suit. Wet Your Pants in Our Three-*

Button Model Elegantly Tailored in Our Own Work-rooms.

"Yes, I do, Lee," the general sales manager said, "but I never saw this."

"It's your business to see it, Pat." Lee looked at me. He had bright blue eyes under white eyebrows and he looked a little like a mean Santa Claus.

"Boone," he said to me, "what's the company policy on selling to Negroes?"

"We discourage it," I said.

"Then why do you have a picture of one of our agents delivering one of our policies to a Negro couple in this month's *Pulse?*"

"I was reading that copy you had me write for your speech to the Life Underwriters Council. That part about it being not only the right of every American to have life insurance protection, but the obligation of every life insurance professional to provide that protection. I thought you were including jigaboos."

Lee bent forward toward me over his desk. "There will be no racial slurs in this office, or, by God, in this company. We do not encourage the sale of life insurance to Negro men and women because they are a poor business risk. Was that explained to you?"

I nodded.

Lee looked at the general sales manager. "Was it, Pat?"

Pat sat very straight in his chair. "Absolutely, Lee. I checked on that personally with Bill Reardon and he told me that Walt Waters had absolutely touched base with Boone on that score. No question about it."

"It has nothing to do with race or with racial prejudice," Lee said. "It is a simple matter of dollars and cents, Boone."

I nodded. The general sales manager said, "Absolutely."

Lee eased back in his chair. "Boone," he said. "I was your age once. I know how you feel. You're full of piss and vinegar about equality, and I admire that. But when you're older you'll come to see that you can't run a business on theory. When the Negroes become acceptable actuarial risks, I'll be the first one to say, 'Sell 'em, and keep selling 'em.'" Lee smiled at me. He was probably an excellent actuarial risk. Unless they rated you for being a blow. "Okay?" he said.

I nodded.

"So, let's not have any more foul-ups, Pat," Lee said.

"Roger," Pat said.

"Wasn't his fault, anyway," I said. "I slipped it by him on purpose."

Lee smiled some more. "That's behind us," Lee said. "Water under the dam." He leaned briskly forward. "Let's get back to work," he said. The general sales manager and I got up and went out.

As I waited for the elevator the general sales manager said, "It was pretty decent of you to take the blame." His voice was full of wonder.

I shrugged. "It was my fault," I said.

"Lee can come down pretty hard," the general sales manager said.

I nodded. The elevator came. I got in. The general sales manager said, "Well, let's get to it. Let's get this thing oiled up." He walked down the hall toward his office with walls and a ceiling (only a little smaller than

Lee's) with a spring in his step. I went down in the elevator.

Dear Jennifer,

There is very little room in the corporate world for dignity. I saw the second- or third-ranking guy in a major corporation sweating with fear over a minor mistake because the president was scolding him. I suppose because he's making a lot of money he then has a lot to lose by getting fired and so has more reason to be scared than I do. But it seemed more like he was simply scared that the boss was mad, the way a timid little kid is in elementary school, afraid of the teacher getting mad, not of what the teacher will do. I have a lot of trouble caring about the corporate goals . . . which are, after all, to make money for the stockholders. Probably a fine ambition, but I don't really give a shit about the stockholders, and in fact, in my heart, I kind of want the corporation to lose.

I love you

CHAPTER
SEVENTEEN

I was working on a promotional page in *Pulse*. The headline on my promotional page read, "1955 Is a $ales $ellabration = $ell Like $ixty in '55." The artwork was an oversized insurance agent with a briefcase under his arm, driving a tiny car at a high speed along a winding road made of dollar bills. At the end of the road was a Miami Beach moorish-castle hotel labeled 1955 SALES CONFERENCE: MIAMI. While I was admiring this, Walt Waters came to my desk, putting on his suit jacket as he walked, and asked me to go into Bill Reardon's office. Reardon was the Director comma Advertising, Public Relations, and Sales Promotion. His office was twice as large as Walt's (exactly—I had measured them both one night when I worked late and no one was around), and the partition walls were twelve inches higher. In the safety of his office Bill had his coat off and his shirt cuffs turned up. But his tie was still snugged up to his collar and his coat was close. At the first sign of a superior he could whip down the cuffs and slip on the coat.

Walt and I sat down. Walt's chair, I noticed, was nearer to Bill's side of the desk than mine.

"Boone, we've got some problems," Bill said. He looked at Walt.

Walt said, "You are a hell of a creative guy, Boone. I mean that, a hell of a creative guy."

"But," Bill said, "you're not fitting in."

I nodded.

Bill had a page of lined yellow paper on the desk in front of him. He glanced at it. "Last October you went out to Secaucus to do a picture story on the district office out there and showed up wearing neither suit coat nor tie." He looked at me and raised his eyebrows.

I nodded.

He looked at his paper again. "And you ran the picture of the Negroes without clearing it with Walt, or me, or Pat Jones."

I nodded. I had a sense where this was going.

"You refused to work on the United Fund campaign."

Nod.

"And now"—Bill looked up from his list and looked full at me. Mr. District Attorney—"we have the year-end listing of conference qualifiers and there's a dozen mistakes in middle initials, spelling of last names, district office codes . . ." He shook his head.

Walt said, "It's just not enough to be creative, Boone."

"Boone," Bill Reardon said, "we're going to have to let you go."

I shrugged and stood up.

"You want to say anything, Boone, in your—ah—defense?" Walt said.

I shook my head. "Nope," I said.

"You're just going to leave like that?"

"Yeah."

"You've got two weeks pay coming, Boone."

I pointed my index finger toward the sky and made a circular motion. "Whoopee," I said.

Dear Jennifer,

Getting fired is more depressing than I thought it would be. I hated the place and had no respect for it, or the people in it, but when they decide they don't want you there, somehow it makes you feel undesirable, or wanting, valueless, maybe. But, anyway, it's done. Too bad I didn't protest about the Negro business, or something dignified, matter of principle, you know? But I got fired for being careless and sloppy in proofreading a list. It's hard to be proud of that. On the other hand, how can I care about anything, let alone the middle initial of some meatball in Newburgh, New York, who sold a million dollars worth of life insurance? The scary thing is that I don't see how I'll be able to care about anything, ever, except you, and you're gone. What will I do? I don't want to get ahead. I want to go back.

I love you

CHAPTER
EIGHTEEN

I had been lunching on ketchup soup at the Automat for a couple of days when I finally got a job with a company called Conray in Cleveland. Conray advanced me the plane fare. I stiffed my landlord two months rent, spent most of the plane fare on beer, and hitchhiked to Parma with ten bucks to my name. I was a tech writer. We were supposed to be writing maintenance manuals for maintenance equipment used to service a solid-fuel missile called Cardinal. Neither the missile nor the maintenance equipment had been built yet, and we were supposed to write the manuals by reading blueprints and schematics and engineering drawings. Nobody in my technical writing group knew how to read them. My supervisor was a Negro named Earl Toomy, who had once been a junior high school science teacher and understood the task at hand no better than I did. I had been hired because I had technical training in the army, though my mastery of international Morse code never did prove useful in understanding a stepdown transformer. Earl decided that we should go to Redstone Arsenal in Huntsville, Ala-

bama, one week, and he got us travel advances and reserved the company plane and had the conference and
travel department reserve us rooms at the Redstone Holiday Inn. I never knew exactly why we were supposed to
be going. When we registered at the Holiday Inn the
desk clerk explained to us with some courtesy that it was
against Alabama law to domicile whites and Negroes
under the same roof. He said it the way you would tell
someone that it was illegal to keep chickens in a hotel
room. Earl complained, which in retrospect was probably
what we went down there for. The argument escalated to
include middle- and upper-level management of Conray,
and concluded when the plant supervisor told me to rent
a car and drive Earl immediately to the nearest free state.
Conray knew the makings of an incident when they saw
one. I thought it would make more sense to get on a com-
mercial airline plane and go back to Cleveland. Earl
agreed, and we landed in Cleveland at 11:15 that night
drunker than three goats. The Conray people fired Earl
for some other official reason shortly thereafter, but they
thought I was a hero, like I'd saved the company from
scandal. They promoted me. Being a group leader made
it easier to conceal the fact that I didn't have any idea
what I was doing. There was some strain in not knowing,
but it was alleviated a bit by the fact that as far as I
could tell nobody knew what he was doing. It struck me
that I may have stumbled upon life's mainspring. *Adams's
Law,* I wrote in Jennifer's journal. *Nobody knows what
the fuck he's doing.* It might be the law of nature.

One Tuesday morning I woke up with a brutal hangover and didn't go to work. I stayed in bed and read the

Plain Dealer and drank beer and ate some bologna sandwiches and watched the Indian game on TV. I liked that
so much I did it the next day and then the next, and by
Friday I'd stayed out too long without calling in to explain what had happened and I realized I'd quit. The
rent was due on my room, so I left without paying and
took a bus to Cincinnati.

I was working in a machine shop near the river and
being trained. Until I was trained I couldn't join the
union and until I joined the union I couldn't actually
make anything usable on the machines. So all day I made
useless pieces of metal—zigzag shapes, donuts, rhom-
boids, and crescents—on the jig borers and metal lathes
and evenings I got drunk, and ate four-way chili if I had
any money left over.

Just before Thanksgiving I was working a metal
lathe and sneaking a few drinks from a hip flask and it
seemed like it would be funny to make a three-foot metal
dildo. It was funny, but no one knew it except me. The
shop super fired me, and called me a goddamned pervert.
I didn't get to keep the dildo either. In Chicago I worked
in a Coca-Cola bottling plant on the south side near
Comiskey Park. I was drunk most of the time. I was okay
loading the trucks; I'd done it before during summer va-
cation from school. It didn't take precision, but the fine
motor work on the production line needed more sobriety
than I was bringing to work. The shipper found out I'd
worked in a Coke plant before and moved me up to the
production line. I was the relief man, filling in for the
people on break, so that every fifteen minutes I moved to

a different spot on the line, until my break came. The job I liked best was screening the bottles. You sat and watched the empty bottles rattle by on the conveyor as they came out of the washer. They passed against a brightly lit white background and you kept a sharp eye peeled to detect any foreign substance in there, like the legendary mouse, or that's what you were supposed to do. I rested. It was the casing table that gave me trouble. The full bottles of Coke came off the line onto a rotating table in black identical procession and piled up. The job was to take them, three in each hand, and put them into the crosshatched wooden cases twenty-four to the case and shove the full case onto the final run out to the stackers. If I caught that job early in the day, before I was too drunk, I could manage it, but once I got to it after lunch. The bottles began to pile up all at once and after five minutes I got dizzy and sat down on a low stack of cases and closed my eyes and waited till the dizziness stopped. The line kept its implacable progress and before the dizziness stopped there were broken bottles and newly made Coca-Cola in a sharp-edged sticky swamp all over the area.

In Dallas I worked a couple of nights washing dishes in the kitchen of a Mexican restaurant on McKinney Street. It was hot and I didn't show up the third night. Instead I took a six-pack and sat in the gravel slope beneath an underpass off Elm Street and blanked my mind the way I did and felt the beer seep into me. I was on my fourth beer of that six-pack when a man scrambled over the guard rail above and stumbled down the side of the overpass and started to take a leak with his forehead pressed against the cement and his feet backed off and braced to keep himself steady. Even then he swayed and before he was finished urinating he slid down the wall and passed out in the recently created mud. I looked at him. His left arm stretched out toward me was in the small splash of light that spilled from the headlamps of his car parked with the motor running on the road above. He wore a wristwatch. Maybe it was expensive. Maybe the guy was rich. I drank some more beer. I got up and walked over toward him, my feet sliding a little in the gravel. Only that left arm was lighted. Above in the dark the cars swooshed by; the man's car motor still idled. Faintly I could hear music from his car radio, hillbilly stuff. I stood looking down at him. He wore a suit. I poked him with my toe. He didn't move. I squatted down and shook his shoulder. "You okay?" I said. He groaned a little and burrowed his head into the wet gravel. I patted his hip pocket and took out his wallet. A flashlight beam hit me with a force that was almost physical. I squinted into it.

A voice said, "Boy, you put both your hands on top of your head and don't you make another move."

I let the wallet drop and put my hands on my head. Behind the blinding light was a Dallas cop with his gun out. He made me lie flat while he patted me down, then he let me sit up.

"You rolling this man, boy?"

"No, I was looking in his wallet to see who he was. I was going to call somebody."

"Mmm."

The cop was feeling the artery pulse in the man's neck.

"He came down to take a leak and passed out," I said.

"And you down here sipping a few cool ones and looking at the dirt. That right?"

"Yeah."

"Where you live?"

"I don't live in Dallas. I was just passing through."

"Got money?"

"I got five bucks," I said.

The cop holstered his gun. "Boy," he said. "You was going to roll this man, and we both know that. But I don't guarantee the night court judge will believe it, and I got a lot to do tonight, including getting this gentleman out of the gully here, and getting his car off the road. So you get up on that highway and start walking west, toward Fort Worth, and if I ever see you in Dallas I'll slam your ass in jail. On sight."

I scrambled up the gravel bank and started walking. It tended to fuse after that. A flat-bed truck hauling chickens. A railroad station in Santa Fe where I was two days before they kicked me out. A woman at night in a park telling me to go home and sober up. A drunk tank where some guy kept crying for Betty. Brackish water in a ditch, motionless white-faced cattle, Hershey bars and day-old bread, the taste of Four Roses whiskey from the neck of a quart bottle passed around in a Quonset hut outside Tacoma. I was picking cranberries by hand, not even a scoop, five cents a box. At night on the bare mattress on the folding iron cot the medicinal cheap whiskey was all there was. All of us drank it, men and women. All of us slept in the Quonset and used the latrine out back. The teenage Indian girl next to me slept every night in a

man's workshirt and by morning it was often twisted up
around her waist. I looked at her pelvis blankly when I
woke up in the morning. She had good thighs and a nice
slope to her belly, but I was living so slightly and so deep
inside that nothing much got through to the reduced
quick of me. That night, though, when the whiskey was
burning my throat and warming my stomach, I asked her
to go out back and we copulated on the ground near the
latrine without any talk at all. She was simply passive except when I was in her; then she humped up and down
as if she were trying to buck me off. I had been a long
time without sex, and the first time, I ejaculated quickly.
She wiped herself between her legs with the bottom of
her cotton dress and we went back into the Quonset.
Most of the pickers were Indian, with some Negroes and
a couple of Chicanos. I was the only white. After that we
used to copulate most nights, but I had a lot of trouble
ejaculating and usually had to roll off finally because I
was exhausted. She would hump steadily until that time
and stop the minute I did, and get up and go in without
comment. I don't know how long I was there, stooped
over all day, drinking and humping at night. We took
turns buying the bottle and passed it around in the fields
during the day. It was shared without question and without reservation, and when it was gone, the man whose
turn it was would get another one. The women weren't
expected to buy one, though they could drink as much as
the men. Usually we'd nurse it, keeping a kind of steady
buzz on all day, and not get really washed away until
nighttime so we could sleep. Sometimes I would miscal-
culate and get drunk too soon and have to head back to
the Quonset early, reeling as I went, to pass out on my

mattress. On nights like that the things I wrote to Jennifer in the journal were barely legible, and very often made no sense.

A fly woke me. It buzzed and hummed as it circled my face, and then was silent when it landed. I could feel it walking along my cheek toward the flare of my right nostril. I brushed it away. The fly buzzed again and hummed as it flew. As I became conscious I could feel how hot I was, and how wet I was with sweat. I opened my eyes stiffly and saw a strange place. My head ached, I was thirsty, and as I shifted slightly, my whole body felt trembly. I rubbed my forehead with the back of my hand. I looked at my hand. The fingernails were dirty and there was a scratch along the back of it that had a ragged scab on it. The fly came back and walked on my face again. I brushed at it and it flew a short distance away, and someone next to me slapped at it. I looked around. I was lying on a cement floor against a cinder block wall in the corner of a room with ten or twelve other men in it. Across the front wall were bars. I was in the drunk tank; I knew what a drunk tank looked like. I'd been in one before. How about this one? Had I been in this one before? No. I had never seen this one before. I didn't know where I was. Across the room somebody was having the dry heaves in the single seatless hopper. I edged my way upright against the wall. A Mexican-looking guy next to me was smoking. I tapped my two fingers against my lips in a smoking gesture. The Mexican looked at me and looked away. The smell of his smoke made me want a cigarette badly. I felt in my pockets. There were no cigarettes. In fact there was nothing at all in my pockets. After a while a guard came and let us all out. They gave me back the tattered mass of notebooks that I kept, and we trooped down a long corridor and out onto a hot sunny street. It was a street I'd never seen. I didn't know where I was. I walked down the hill in the heat. At a newsstand I saw the *Los Angeles Times* for sale, and the *Herald Examiner*. I was in L.A. and my last memory was a thousand miles north and five days ago. I felt shaky and sick. In a store window I saw my reflection. My hair was stringy and long; my face was half covered with a scruffy beard. One sleeve of my shirt was gone and the zipper on my fly was broken. My pants gaped. There were no laces in my shoes, which made it harder to walk, and as I moved away from the window I shuffled. I needed a drink. I needed cigarettes. I panhandled. By evening I'd gotten nearly a dollar and a half's worth of change. I bought a pack of Camels and a bottle of port wine, and sat on a bench in a park off Broadway in downtown L.A. and smoked and drank my wine. After half a bottle I felt pretty decent. I studied my pants. I tried to figure out what they had been when I got them. I wasn't even sure they were mine. They seemed big in the waist. They were so dirty that I couldn't tell what color they were. The knee was ripped. I looked at my shirt. It might once have been khaki. Maybe an army shirt. I couldn't tell. I sipped my wine, trying to make it last. The weather got a little cooler after it got dark. Somebody sat next to me on the bench. I gave her a cigarette. She had a bottle of muscatel, full. I gave her a sip of my port. She gave me some muscatel.

"Cops hassle you here?" I said.

"Nope, not if you're quiet. They let you sleep."

I nodded.

She said, "I know where there's another bottle. You want me to get it?"

I said yes.

She said, "You let me have some of your smokes?"

"Yes."

She was gone a bit and then she was back. She had a jug of sherry. We drank it all and smoked most of the Camels. Late in the night on the grass by the bench I remembered fumbling under her clothes.

The sun hit me full face when it rose. I was lying on my back. My shirt was still on, but my pants were off and I was exposed. She was undressed, too, her dress pulled up under her armpits, nothing on underneath. She was fat and there was grime in all the creases of her body. She had a pimple inside her left thigh and her toenails were long and dirty and broken. She was lying on her side with one arm across my chest. There was dried vomit on her face and on my chest and neck. She slept with her mouth open. Some of her teeth were missing, and a line of saliva drooled down and mixed with the vomit. Above me the bright blue sky was cloudless and the early sun was bright as it rolled in from the east. There was dew on the grass and all of me ached. I inched out from under her fat blue-veined arm and sat up. There was dried semen matting my pubic hair. I struggled upright and pulled my pants up. There were other derelicts sleeping all over the park. I began to walk. As I walked, the tears began to trail down my face and my breath came in the short gasps you get when you start to cry. A clock in a building showed ten minutes past five. I walked until I came to Wilshire Boulevard. Somewhere I had read that Wilshire ran all the way to the ocean. I walked along it, crying. When I came to a bench I sat on it. In MacArthur Park I sat for a while under a tree and rested. I reached Santa Monica about the time people were going home for supper, cars full of men in suits and hats, dressed-up young women, usually three or four to the car. Now and then someone would look at me, my dirty face streaked with tear lines, my clothes crusted and torn, my pace slow, bent, wobbly. They would always look away. I kept going, slowly, shaky, and desperate for a drink. I had smoked my last cigarette in MacArthur Park a long time ago. I ached for another one. Crying made my nose run and the mucus had dried in my unshaven mustache. I kept moving and there was the ocean. I had gone as far as I could. I sat down on the beach, and then lay back. I used the journal notebooks for a pillow and lay still with tears still flowing as the sun that had wakened me this morning, set out ahead of me, flooding the Pacific with its rose benediction, and then it sank from sight, as I had, and the darkness came and no one could see me.

CHAPTER
NINETEEN

"Conduct," Scott Fitzgerald had written, "may be founded on the hard rock or the wet marshes." The phrase was with me as I woke at sunrise. I sat smelling and crusted, with sand layered over the dirt and vomit, the nasal drainage and the dried semen, and thought about the phrase and about *The Great Gatsby* and marveled at how it could come back through the years since I'd read it, just like that, as clear as if I'd read it this morning. "Conduct may be founded on the hard rock or the wet marshes." I got to my feet unsteadily with my body shrieking for a drink and my throat clenched with the desire for a cigarette. In front of me the Pacific was calm in the early light and entirely empty to the horizon. I felt my stomach turn. I sank to my knees, then hands and knees, and vomited. There wasn't much down there, so not much came up. But it took a long time. When it was over I felt dizzy. I crawled toward the ocean and then got to my feet and walked toward it and into it. There was night chill to it and the shock of it centralized me a little. I kept moving as the water came up over my thighs and then sat down in the water, neck-deep a yard from shore. The silence seemed to stretch up to the arch of sky and echo back. My wet clothes seemed to be shrinking in on me and I tore them off and threw them from me toward the open sea, shoes and all. I had a sort of a festered sore on my stomach and the salt water stung it sharply. The sensation was one of the first I'd felt, and I liked it. I began to take handfuls of clean, fine sand from the sea floor and scrub myself with it, scouring my face and hair and body with it, and as I felt the faint tingle of it where the sand scraped my skin and the salt water worked on it, I began to scour harder, all over, everywhere, again and again. I sank my face and head underwater and scrubbed it with the sand and then rinsed it with violent rubbing. For maybe an hour, until the sun was full above the horizon, I scrubbed and rinsed until my body was sanded clean. I gargled with seawater again and again, and finally dove beneath the sea and stayed under as long as I could, rolling slowly in the water. When I could stay under no longer, I stood up with my wet hair plastered to my scalp and the water streaming off my body. Conduct had been too long in the marshes. I stared at the shore and beyond it, eastward across the almost endless range of the republic toward Jennifer. *I will get you back,* I said. *You will be the rock.*

To my right was a small pier and on one of the pilings someone had left a bathing suit to dry. I waded over and stole it. Up close it turned out to be a pair of cut-off jeans and not really a bathing suit. So much the better. They were a little large, but they covered me. I walked back and retrieved my journal, a collection of cardboard-covered notebooks packaged together with string. They were dog-eared and stained, but I had hung on to them since I'd begun them, even when the blackout periods started coming. It struck me that I didn't know how long I'd been keeping them because I didn't know what year it was. I couldn't even remember the date I'd seen on the newspaper yesterday—or was it the day before? The sun was high enough now to dry me. The sore on my stomach looked clean for the first time in months. It had started as a simple boil. I walked up the beach and across a short stretch of grass to the road that ran along the water. I had no money. I was on my second day without a drink or a smoke. In the daylight my bare upper body was thin and flabby. *Hard to be both,* I thought. *Takes a lot of careful planning to be skinny and fat together.* My forearms and hands and face and neck were tan; the rest of me was grayish-white except the pinkish flare of the sore on my stomach. But I was clean. I found a newspaper in a trash barrel that said it was September 12, 1961. I was twenty-nine.

In the window of a coffee shop a hand-lettered cardboard sign said KITCHEN HELP WANTED—INQUIRE WITHIN. Outside, a bulky man in a clean white T-shirt was hosing down his sidewalk. There were tattoos on both forearms, blue with red highlights. Snakes and knives, and nude women.

I said, "I know I look weird, but I was sleeping on the beach two nights ago and somebody stole everything I had, car, wallet, clothes, razor, everything."

The bulky man said, "Yeah?" He had graying dark

hair cut very short, and his face glistened from his morning shave. His fingernails were square and clean. There
was a wedding ring on his left hand.

"I need a job. Would you hire me?"

The bulky man swept the hose back and forth carefully in front of the shop, washing yesterday's trash inch
by inch toward the gutter.

"What's that?" he said, nodding at my journal.

"I'm trying to be a writer," I said.

He nodded again. The stream from the hose moved
the last line of leaves and papers over the curb.

"Wash dishes?" he said.

"Sure."

"Okay," he said. "I'll hire you by the day. You work
out today, I'll hire you back tomorrow."

"Okay."

"Buck and a half an hour and meals. I pay you at the
end of the day."

I nodded.

"You want breakfast. I got the grill on. We open at
seven."

I said, "What time is it?"

He looked at his watch. "Six twenty."

Inside the coffee shop the bulky man said, "Tom
Hernandez."

I said, "Boone Adams." We extended hands. His grip
was hard and the muscles in his bare arm bunched as we
shook.

Tom cooked scrambled eggs on the grill and I ate
them with toast, and drank coffee thick with cream and
sugar. I turned down bacon. My stomach was edgy and I

didn't want to try it too soon. I couldn't remember the last time I'd eaten from a plate.

Tom lit a cigarette and the smell of the smoke made my stomach tighten. He offered me one. I shook my head.

"Don't smoke?" he said.

"Trying to quit," I said. I hadn't realized that I was until I said it.

When the first customers came at seven I was in the kitchen at a deep pair of set tubs. The dirty dishes were shoved through a small opening at one end of the counter and I washed them in one sink and rinsed them in another and let them drain in a big rack on the drainboard. The dishes during the breakfast rush came faster than I could wash them, but I kept enough clean so they could keep serving. Tom's wife worked the counter and Tom ran the grill. He did eggs or pancakes with bacon, ham, or sausage, and home fries on the grill along with English muffins and toast, which he did eight slices at a time in a big old silver pop-up toaster. The coffee he drew from a big silver urn. Fruit juice was canned. After nine the breakfast rush dwindled and I caught up on the dishes in time for lunch. At 11:15 I took ten minutes and had a ham and cheese sandwich on rye bread and two glasses of milk. Lunch was mostly sandwiches plus hamburgers or grilled cheese. The dishes were easier to clean. Tom closed at three o'clock in the afternoon. I finished washing up at 4:30.

"I only pay you for the hours I'm open," Tom said. "Otherwise you could stall around till midnight."

I nodded. He gave me a ten and two ones. My legs ached with exhaustion.

"There's some sandwiches made up and left over in the icebox," Tom said. "Where you sleeping tonight?"

"On the beach."

Tom said, "Wait a minute." He went out through the back door and came back in two minutes with one of those folding plastic mattresses that fit in the back of station wagons. He put it on the floor in the kichen in front of the sink. "You want to sleep here?"

"Yeah," I said. "I'd appreciate it."

"If you go out, make sure the door's locked. Key's on a nail behind the shutter on the left." He showed me.

"What size shoes you take?" Tom said.

"Nine."

"I'm nine and a half, but maybe I got some old sneakers you could have. Board of health would shit if they seen you in here barefoot."

I nodded. My head was woozy and I was so tired I couldn't focus on Tom.

"I took the cash with me," Tom said. "No point looking for any."

"I wouldn't," I said.

"Anyone would," Tom said. "I'll be in around six to get ready for breakfast."

I put the twelve dollars in my pocket. Enough for three cases of beer, twenty bottles of Pastene port. I could imagine the beer going in and seeping through me, washing clear and clean into all the parched cells. In my imagination my body tautened and enlarged like a watered plant, revitalizing like a dried sponge dipped into a spring. I could get a couple of six-packs and put them in the freezer to get really chilled and I could lie on the mattress here and drink them and be whole again. It seemed a long walk to the store. I was head-swimming tired. I could rest a little, then get up and get the beer. I lay down on the mattress, and fell asleep with the late afternoon sun shining on the wall above my head.

CHAPTER
TWENTY

I woke up soaked with sweat in the small hot kitchen.
The sun still shone in through the window, but it was on
the opposite wall. I looked at the clock above the counter
in the front of the shop: 5:40. Another day without a
drink or a smoke. Two days? Three? I couldn't quite be
sure. I got up and got some bar soap from the lavatory
and walked down to the beach. I stripped off my clothes
and waded in and washed with the soap. It didn't lather
much in the salt water, but it got the sweat off. I put my
stolen jeans back on over my damp body and walked
back up to the coffee shop. I got the key from behind the
shutter and let myself in. I ate a leftover tuna sandwich
and drank milk. Then I opened up the front door to let
the air in and found the mop and a bucket and washed
down the floor. Tom arrived while I was at it. He gave
me a pair of white Keds and a clean white T-shirt. The
sneakers were a little big and the T-shirt, one of Tom's,
was very big, but at least I was covered. Tom showed me
how to get the big coffee urn ready and started for the

day. He showed me how to turn on the grill and how to get the deep fryer going. I had two cups of coffee before the first customers arrived at seven and I started washing dishes.

After that I had everything ready to go in the morning by the time Tom got to the shop and after three days he took to coming a little later. After five days I had sixty dollars in my pocket. I got a haircut, bought a razor and a toothbrush and some salt-water soap. I hadn't had a drink or a cigarette since I'd started with Tom.

Tom closed Mondays, and I had my first day off. I took a bus downtown and bought myself a pair of chino pants and white shirt with a button-down collar. Then I went back to the shop and got my journal and sat on the beach to write in it. I hadn't written in a while and I started to reread a little to pick up the thread. The journal was a mess. There were stains on it from ketchup and pickle juice and grease, and spilled beer or wine. The pages were soiled and creased and wrinkled, all of them were ripped, and some were nearly torn in two. Much of it was barely legible. As I looked at it my eyes filled until the pages were bleary in front of me. I wiped them clear. *Okay,* I said, *okay. I'll start with this.* I got up and walked back to the shop and put the journal on a shelf above the sink. Then I went out and down the block to a dime store and bought a dozen spiral-bound notebooks and four ball-point pens. Then I went back to the shop and sat at the counter and began to rewrite the journal.

Every morning I went down and bathed in the sea and as the weeks went by and I kept saving money, I added another pair of pants and another shirt and two T-shirts and a pair of sneakers to my wardrobe. Every after-

noon after the shop closed I sat at the counter for an hour
and restored the journal, printing painstakingly because
my handwriting was messy. It had been a month and a
half since I'd had a drink or smoked a cigarette. I was
going to sleep at nine o'clock at night and eating three
meals a day and putting on weight. One morning before I
bathed in the ocean I jogged a little ways along the
beach until I got tired. It wasn't very far. But the next
morning I did it again, and the next morning I went a little farther. By December I was running three miles a
morning and had dropped ten pounds.

For Christmas Tom and his wife gave me a six-
month membership in the Santa Monica YMCA. And
Tom, who worked out there regularly, took me down and
showed me how to lift weights. I could barely bench-
press seventy-five pounds that first day, but Tom didn't
laugh at me, and I went with him every other afternoon
after work, before I wrote in my journal.

From the time I woke up until I finished writing my
journal in the late afternoon I was fine. Running, working, lifting weights, re-creating the journal, occupied my
mind. But by six o'clock I had finished the journal and
eaten my supper and cleaned up the dishes and it would
be three or four hours before I'd fall asleep. In that time
it was hard not to drink and hard not to smoke.

I went over to the branch library in Santa Monica
and took out a card and brought home a copy of The
Great Gatsby. I read it in two evenings, and reread it in
two more. The quote I remembered hadn't meant quite
what I'd remembered it as meaning, but it was true in
spirit to the book. I was startled at how good the book
was. Grinding through it in sophomore English survey, I

hadn't realized. Then I went back and got *Go Down, Moses* by Faulkner and read "The Bear" and found myself nearly breathless at some of the writing. As the evenings unfolded I read Hemingway and Steinbeck and Dos Passos. I read *Moby Dick* and *The Scarlet Letter*, and *Walden* and *The Ambassadors* and *Hamlet* and *King Lear* and *Othello*. I read *Othello* in one of those casebook editions for colleges and read the essays also. It led me to literary criticism and I read Richard Sewall on tragedy and Tillyard on the Elizabethan world picture and Lovejoy on the great chain of being. I read R.W.B. Lewis and Henry Nashe Smith and then I read *Walden* twice more. I read books on nutrition and I read *The New York Times* and *The Boston Globe* and the L.A. papers, the *Times* and the *Herald Examiner*.

I was up to five miles along the curve of the beach every morning, and doing two-hundred-pound bench presses and working on the last ten pages of my journal restoration when Tom told me he was closing the shop.

"They're going to buy the whole business block and tear it up and rebuild the fucker," he told me while we were at the Y. "I got a job cooking at a place in Torrance."

I nodded. "That's tough, Tom, to have the thing sold out from under you."

He shrugged. "Don't matter. I'll probably make more cooking for somebody else. What about you?"

"I got five hundred bucks put away," I said. "It'll hold me till I find something."

That night I finished rewriting my journal and packed the six neatly filled-in spiral notebooks in the bottom of my gym bag. I put my extra pants and shirt in on top of them, and my shaving stuff and toothbrush wrapped in aluminum foil. Then I read *The Big Sleep* until bedtime.

In the morning I said good-bye to Tom and his wife. The wife, who hadn't said twenty words to me in seven months, cried and hugged me and kissed me on the mouth.

I said to Tom, "I think I might have died if I hadn't seen you last fall washing off the sidewalk."

Tom nodded. "You've come a way," he said. We shook hands, and I left them closing up the shop and headed for Colorado Street. On the corner I stopped and looked at myself in the black glass facade of a drugstore. I was wearing jeans and a T-shirt. I was tanned from my morning runs and my stomach was flat. I weighed 170 pounds and my biceps stretched the sleeves of the T-shirt. Tom was right. I'd come a way. But I had a way left.

I walked up to Wilshire and caught a bus downtown.

CHAPTER
TWENTY-ONE

I got a one-room furnished apartment with kitchenette and bath in a building in Hollywood on Franklin Avenue near Kenmore. The day I moved in I went to Ralph's market on Sunset and bought groceries and made myself steak and salad with French bread. I bought a bottle of red wine to go with the meal. It had been eight months since I had had a drink. It was time to find out. I drank two glasses of the wine with my meal, and sipped the rest of the bottle afterward while I read the *Times* and the *Herald Examiner* classified pages, looking for a job. There were three openings for a carpenter's helper and I marked them for the morning. Then I washed up the dishes and went to bed with a mild buzz and a full stomach.

I could still taste wine in my mouth the next morning and my head ached enough to take aspirin with my orange juice. But I didn't feel bad, and I didn't feel like I needed a drink. Maybe next week I could try a couple of beers. I did a careful journal entry after breakfast, and then took a bus downtown to a temporary office in a storefront on the corner of Seventh and Hope to interview for the carpentry job. The job was with a big construction firm that was putting up houses in the Toluca Lake area in North Hollywood. They hired two of us, probably because we were sober, me, and a muscular black man named Roy Washington. A half-hour later we were in the front seat of a pickup truck with a carpenter named Henry Reagan heading for the job.

Henry was a thin, drawn, old man, over sixty, with skin that had weathered to a permanent reddish tone. He wore glasses with gold rims and a sweat-stained baseball cap.

"You know anything about carpentry?"

I said, "No." Washington shook his head.

"You own any tools?"

"No."

"Jesus," Henry said. "How am I supposed to teach you anything if you don't have any motherfucking tools?"

Washington and I looked at each other.

"I'll lend you some, but as soon as you get paid, you sure better buy your own," Henry said. "What'd you boys do before?"

"Boxer," Washington said.

"How come you're not boxing now?" Henry said.

"Can't get no fights," Washington said. "People ducking me. My manager's working on it. But in the meantime I gotta eat."

Henry glanced at me, sitting in the middle between him and Washington.

"How about you? You fight too?"

"Not if I can run," I said. "I was washing dishes in a

place out in Santa Monica. Somebody bought the building and is gonna tear the place down."

Henry nodded, still sidelonging me as he drove.

"You didn't get the upper body rinsing dishes," he said.

"I work out a little."

"You'll be working out a lot more by the time I get through teaching your asses," Henry said.

Washington looked at Henry's narrow arms and winked at me. Henry turned the truck into the dirt road of a construction site and parked in front of a row of newly poured concrete slabs.

"Okay, boys," Henry said. "Time to start learning. I'm going to make first-class fucking framers out of you, and I'm in a hurry."

He didn't succeed by evening of the first day, but neither Washington nor I laughed at the thinness of his arms again. He gave us sixteen-ounce hammers and nailing aprons and we filled the aprons with handfuls of ten-penny nails from a fifty-pound keg that he had in the back of the truck.

"Okay," Henry said. "We're going to frame this house. I'm going to show you how and you're going to do it. You can expect to fuck it up a few times until you get the feel of things. Don't let it bother you. If you do it wrong, I'll straighten it out. Let's get the cocksucker going."

And we did. We built sections of the frame on the floor of the slab, and then raised them into position and nailed them together. Henry could drive a ten-penny nail full in with two strokes of the hammer. Washington and I took ten or twelve bangs apiece to get one in. We bent

half of them. Henry made us pull out any bent ones. He
made us hold the hammer down at the butt end instead
of choking up, and he showed us how to take a full-
armed swing with it instead of small taps.

"Hit the cocksucker," he said. "Two swings and it's
in. No sense tiring yourself out with ten bangs. Let the
hammer do the work; let the weight of the head do it.
You know how to let the head do the work, don't you?"

He was inexhaustible. He drove nails steadily all afternoon, varying it only to cut the studs to size, driving
the circular saw through the wood with a clean, sharp,
single movement. When Washington and I did it the saw
would bind and the smell of friction-seared wood was
sharp.

By five o'clock, when we stopped, Washington and I
were soaked with sweat and my arms were shaking tired.
I had hit myself on the thumb four times. Henry looked
exactly as he had, his thin, reddish body moving with the
same tight alacrity it had when he'd picked us up in the
morning.

"We start at eight," Henry said. "Punch in at the
field shed. If you're late, the foreman will take a bite out
of your fucking ass."

We put the hammers and the aprons in the tool box
in the back of Henry's truck and got in. He drove us
down to Hollywood Boulevard.

"I'm heading for West L.A.," he said. "I'll drop you
boys here."

Washington and I went into a bar on Hollywood
near the corner of Wilton and had a beer. I was so
drained and thirsty, I forgot for a moment that it was the

first beer since last fall. It was cold and it filled me as I had always imagined it would.

"Where you staying?" I asked Washington.

He shrugged. "Around," he said.

I looked at him in the mirror behind the bar. He had a wide mouth and a little mustache like Ray Robinson wore. I didn't see any sign of damage on his face except a horizontal scar maybe two inches along the cheekbone under his right eye.

"You need a place to stay?" I said.

"Naw, man, I'm fine," he said.

"Then how come you're staying 'around,' " I said.

"Don't get too pushy, man," Washington said.

"Why don't you stay with me for a while," I said. "I slept in too many parks to think it's fun."

"Where you staying?" Washington said.

"Up on Franklin Avenue," I said. "Near Kenmore."

His eyes were hazel, with a lot of white around the iris. "They let me in up there?"

"They let me in," I said.

"I ain't the same color as you," Washington said.

"I noticed that," I said. "Let's integrate the fucker."

Washington grinned. He raised his beer glass toward me. "Okay," he said. "Let's do it." So we did.

CHAPTER
TWENTY-TWO

Roy Washington trained in a gym on 103rd Street, near
Alameda on weekends, and sometimes, if we weren't too
tired after work, I went with him and he taught me to
box a little, so that when we sparred, he could get a
workout. The neighborhood was black, and most of the
men in the gym were black, but nobody paid me much
attention, and I felt comfortable enough as long as I was
with Roy. When we weren't working out evenings, we'd
drink a few beers and read. I was the first person Roy
had known socially who had been to college.

"Lucky you flunked out," he told me once, "or I'd
never understand nothing you said."

Race relations were fermenting in the early sixties,
but Roy and I were okay. We did a lot of honky–nigger
humor, taught each other the things we knew (Roy knew
more useful things than I did), and got a chance to ob-
serve firsthand that the great issues often have little to do
with the individual ones.

"I don't want you honkies giving me what I get," Roy

told me one night. "I want to take it." We were at the gym taking turns on the heavy bag on a hot night. The sweat glistened like oil on both our bodies. I was holding the bag, and as Roy hit it, the bag bucked and shuddered against me.

After the workout, showered and dressed, we walked to the bus stop carrying our gym bags, through a populace uniformly black. Hazel eyes looking at me without response.

"How you feel walking around Watts?" Roy said on the bus.

"I wouldn't do it without you," I said.

"Good idea," he said.

"Even with you," I said, "I feel, you know, alien. Like I don't know the score."

"I feel that way most of the time," Roy said. "Laws and marches and stuff don't seem to change that."

"So what will change it?" I said. "So what can we do?"

"We?" Roy grinned. "Who the fuck you talking for? You white folks?"

"Aren't you speaking for the coons?" I said.

"I'm speaking for me," he said. "I ain't trying to change anything. I'm trying to get a good life going. I'm trying to make money, and I'm trying to take no shit from anybody."

I nodded. "Yeah. I understand that," I said. "The 'we' was asshole."

Roy looked at me next to him on the bus. "You already done what you can do."

I got to be a good framer that summer, and a decent all-purpose carpenter. I learned enough about fist fighting to go three rounds with Roy without getting badly hurt. Though I always wore the headgear and Roy never really aired it out. I was able to drink three or four beers a night and stop. I was able to do it and not smoke. When I could, I still lifted some weights at the Y. Roy and I ran in Griffith Park some mornings before work. I had a book on nutrition from the library. I worked on eating right and every night I tried to read at least a couple of chapters in something worth reading. Roy did most of those things with me.

In early June I met a girl, a librarian that I got talking to as I checked out *The Portable Faulkner*. I was on my way home from work wearing work shoes and jeans, a sweaty T-shirt and a Dodgers baseball cap. The hammer holster was still attached to my belt.

"Have you read Faulkner before?" she said.

"Yeah, I've read *Sartoris, Intruder in the Dust*," I said. "And *Knight's Gambit*, and *Pylon* and 'The Bear.'"

She had longish honey-colored hair and a slim figure. She wore a frilly white shirt with a round collar and a black bow tie, sort of. Her fingernails were short and pointed and done in a neutral polish.

"Well, I'll be damned," she said.

"Can't judge a book by its cover," I said.

She smiled. "Let that be a lesson to me," she said.

After that we used to joke about her assumption every time I went in, and one night near closing, I said, "Would you care to get something to eat, or a drink, after work?"

She said she would and we did. Her name was Patti Wyman. After that I saw her at least two nights a week. Sometimes Roy would get a date and we'd go to a

Dodger game. Sunday afternoons Patti and I would go to the L.A. County Art Museum and then we'd walk up Fairfax afterward and snack at the Farmers Market.

On the Fourth of July Patti borrowed her father's car and we drove over Mulholland Drive into Griffith Park. We found a place with no one around and spread out our blanket and took out our cooler and our portable radio and the big picnic basket that belonged to Patti's mother that Patti and her mother had packed. There was a shrimp and avocado salad, assorted finger sandwiches, cheese and fruit, and sangria and Mexican beer in the cooler. We listened to the radio and ate and drank and washed up with little scented towelettes packed in foil that Patti's mother saved from whenever she went to restaurants that gave them out.

The Dodgers were playing a doubleheader and we listened to three innings of it lying quietly under a tree when Patti said, "We've gone out about twelve times now and you haven't even kissed me."

"I'm shy with girls," I said. "Should I do it now?"

"Yes."

Her breath smelled of wine as I leaned over her and her mouth was open as I kissed her. The kiss got longer and her body arched up toward me a little. I heard myself groan a little. Not pain, not joy either. Relief almost, a knot being loosened. I slid my hand under her blouse and she pulled away from me. I took my hand away quickly.

"I'm sorry," I said. My voice was hoarse. "I shouldn't have put my hand on you."

"No," she said. Her face was serious. "That's all right. I just think we ought to undress."

"Here?"

She nodded.

"What if someone sees us?"

"Boonie," she smiled, "it's nineteen sixty-two. People do make love."

I was startled at her body. Naked, it was much more than I had expected. She was as slim as she looked clothed, but her breasts seemed bigger, and her buttocks rounder. As we lay together she traced the muscle line in my chest. "You're very strong-looking," she said. "Are you?"

"I'm getting stronger," I said. We moved our hands gently over each other. There was passion, but there was an air of investigation too.

"Have you done this very often, Boonie?"

"No, not very often," I said. "I'm almost thirty and I haven't had much sex for that age. Whores and stuff in the army mostly."

"I've only done it with one other person before," Patti said.

"Often?"

"Nearly every day for maybe six months," she said. With her arms around me, she rubbed my lower back gently with both hands. "Then we broke up."

"I'm sorry," I said.

"It's all right. It happens. There will be someone else."

I kissed her right breast. "I am not him, Patti," I said.

"I know. That's okay too. This is fun. It doesn't have to be more."

"You should know that," I said. My voice was getting

hoarser. "This doesn't lead anywhere. It can't. It means nothing but what it means now."

"Yes," she said, and kissed me quietly. "I have always known that. It's okay." She leaned back and her thighs relaxed and her mouth opened slightly. She slid her hands up my back and pulled my head down toward her.

We made love for a long time, and it was a great pleasure for both of us. We were slick with sweat and gasping for breath when we finished. I lay still on top of her for a long while and finally rolled off and lay beside her holding her hand. There was a little breeze and it felt cool on my wet body. My eyes felt wet, but I didn't cry except to blink a few tears out so they'd dry.

Patti raised on one elbow and looked at me and smiled. "Unpracticed," she said. "But frolicsome."

"That's the first sex I've ever had that was simply pleasure and without complications."

She ran a forefinger over my forehead and the bridge of my nose. "You seem a little sad," she said.

"I wish it could have been you," I said. "I like you."

"Why don't you tell me about who it is," Patti said.

"First let's get dressed," I said.

"Shy," she said, "prudish maybe."

When we were dressed again I sat with my arm around her and my back against a tree and talked about Jennifer, and me, and the last eight years. I had spoken of it to no one, had organized it, had tried to give it shape only in my journal entries. As I talked to Patti I was often quoting my journal entries. I talked much of the afternoon. Patti listened. The cooler was empty by the time I finished. So was the basket.

"And that quote from Fitzgerald just appeared in my

head," I said. "In context it didn't even mean what I remembered it to mean. But it was what I started back with. 'Conduct may be founded on the hard rock or the wet marshes.' I had to care about something. I had to have a goal. I had to . . ." I gestured with my free hand. After spending so long a time in relative silence, I still had trouble talking.

"What you are doing," Patti said after a small silence, "is really quite remarkable. It is the most committed act of will I've ever seen. What you're doing, whether you think of it this way or not"—her nice face was very serious and she was looking right at me, leaning forward a little and turning her head—"is you're becoming worthy of her. You've set out to create a man she deserves."

There were birds moving in the trees above us, and the scent of something flowering on the breeze. I couldn't think of anything to say.

"My God," Patti said, "she is a lucky woman. I hope she finds it out."

CHAPTER
TWENTY-THREE

One of the things I did regularly was review the Boston papers in the periodical room at the main library, downtown. I had a sense that I ought to stay in touch with things back there, where I assumed she was. She might have moved, of course, but if she had, I had no way to know where, and maybe she hadn't. It was a way of keeping in touch, like the journal.

In the Living section of *The Boston Globe* for August 11, 1962, was a picture of Archibald MacLeish drinking a glass of wine and talking with Professor John Merchent. The name clamored along my nervous system. It was him, and behind him, smiling at someone out of the picture . . . the clamor stilled. Everything stilled. The life in me suspended as I looked at her picture after eight years. I was, I thought afterward, like one of those prey animals, run down by a predator, whose last moments are catatonic as shock obscures both fear and pain. Had a tree fallen, it would have made no sound. Perhaps no movement.

When time began again I read the story. It was short. MacLeish had read poetry at Taft University in Walford, Mass. Merchent was a member of the University Forum Committee. With him was Mrs. Merchent. They were shown at a reception in the faculty club. "Okay," I said out loud. "Okay." No one in the periodical room paid any attention.

It had taken me seven years to get to the West Coast. It took me ten hours to go back east with a year's savings in my pocket. I landed in Boston on a bright thick August morning. And went straight from the airport to Taft. I got a catalogue from the admissions office and read it. Merchent was an assistant professor in the English department. I went back to admissions. It was too late to apply for regular admission. School began in a month, but I could certainly enroll as a special student for the fall semester and meanwhile apply for regular admission in January.

Taft University was suburban Boston. It sat on a tree-shaded campus and looked, in fact, like most colleges look in the catalogue pictures: vines, bricks, grass, paths, fraternity row, the student commons, a chapel with a white spire. I was thirty years and two days old when I walked across the campus at nine in the morning to go to my first class. I was three thousand miles and one year distant from the morning when I woke up in despair on the edge of the Pacific. I was aware of the distance I'd traveled.

By January I was enrolled as a second-semester sophomore at Taft; and in early February the V.A., encouraged by a congressman from my district, restored my G.I. Bill. I did a paper on Eugene O'Neill that got an A

("You write with easy mastery," the professor had commented in red ink at the end), a close reading of Marvell's poem "Bermudas" which got an A— ("Clearly you know how to read, and read ingeniously, perhaps, in this case, a bit too ingeniously"), and a long, seminar paper in Shakespeare's use of comic elements in the tragedies and histories ("You have given yourself, and us, a splendid course, and some genuine insights. A+). I still didn't enjoy school and I still found most of the professors annoying, but my powers of concentration and my ability at self-discipline had enlarged through the years and I took some real pleasure in getting myself into an organized and active relationship with literature and with the past. After school I worked out at the Taft gym, ran the track, and worked three nights a week tending bar at the Holiday Inn on Mass. Avenue in Cambridge.

I had avoided taking Merchent's course, and I had not seen Jennifer. I would do both, I knew, but I approached things in a kind of intuitive sequence, like a recovering heart patient, whose body somehow whispers to him, *This, not that. You're not ready for that.* I saw Merchent several times in the hall, between classes, and looked at him carefully. Still tall, and blond, he had developed a small paunch. The paunch was something you probably noticed more quickly if you felt about him as I did. The eyes were a little pouchy, too, and his tan looked superficial, as if the pallor beneath were enduring, and the outdoor color an affectation. His clothes were splendid, and probably cost more than I had earned all told since last I saw him. And he seemed the darling of the female English majors who often gathered about him as he strolled from class. The graduate students closest to him, the younger women in a descending hierarchy of admirers, on the fringes looking on. The male students in my observation paid him very little heed.

Merchent didn't notice me. He had no reason to. He'd seen me once, eight years ago. I hadn't mattered to him much then. I didn't now. But he mattered to me. Next semester I'd take his course.

The day after Washington's Birthday the English department held a reception for its majors and faculty in the department lounge in Munson Hall. I went and Jennifer was there.

CHAPTER
TWENTY-FOUR

I knew since I came to Taft that I would see her eventually. It was, after all, why I had come. I had steadily developing confidence in my self-control. So I was in some sense ready when it happened.

The room was crowded. There were a lot of students and most of the English faculty. Many of both were smoking and the air was close. People were sipping sherry and eating potato chips with some kind of sour cream dip. There were many more women than men in the student body and about the reverse ratio in the faculty. I got a glass of sherry and sipped it sparingly as I glanced around the room. I always looked for her. I had begun looking for her the moment I got off the plane in Boston. I was where she lived. I might see her anytime. A young woman in a loose blue dress was urging her interpretation of "Sunday Morning" upon a professor wearing a khaki shirt and a flowered tie under his dark gray double-breasted suit. There were cat hairs on the suit, his brown shoes were unshined, and he needed a haircut.

"I would suggest," he was saying, "that the 'ambiguous undulations' which those pigeons make at the end of the poem can be seen to suggest Stevens's own stance."

"But," she said, leaning toward him with her sherry clamped unthought of in her intense fist, "didn't the Holy Ghost appear as a dove?"

"Certainly," he said, and smiled as kindly as he could, "but that doesn't mean . . ."

I moved on. Merchent was there with a number of young women gathered about him. "Wisconsin is excellent," he was saying, "and the University of North Carolina, surprisingly, has a very fine graduate program." All the young women nodded. "Of course," he went on, "Yale is unequaled for its eighteenth-century program. Fred Pottle has done some really fine work down there." The young women nodded again, just as if they knew who Fred Pottle was. I knew that behind the nod most of them were trying to figure out if the eighteenth century was the seventeen hundreds or the eighteen hundreds.

Jennifer was near him but faced away, talking to the chairman of the department. She wore a knit dress of burnt orange, tied at the waist with a soft thin cord. Her hair was done in a French twist, her engagement diamond flashed on her hand as she talked, and her face was as brilliant with animation and life as it had been when I met her. I felt as if I would sink to my knees.

I did not. I stood as motionless and still as I had the first time I had seen her, twelve years before, and let the impact of her wash over me . . . the golden girl . . . the king's daughter . . . the slickness of silk beneath cloth . . . lipstick. The room and people seemed to coalesce around her like one of those children's toys where you look through a viewer and turn the knob and endless patterns form and re-form . . . a jar in Tennessee . . . a magic lantern on the wall . . . I inhaled as deeply as I could and got steadier. The chairman was smiling as he listened, and nodding. He threw back his head to laugh. I moved carefully, as if on a slippery surface, toward them and stood so that when she was through speaking to the chairman she would see me. She wouldn't see me before. I remembered her concentration, and she did but one thing at a time.

I waited with a feeling of trembly exhaustion moving along my arms and legs. It was the same feeling I got when I'd finished squeezing out an extra repetition on the bench, one final shuddering dip on the parallel bars. I took in another deep breath. *Control,* I said to myself, *control.* The word helped me. I clung to it, fixing on it the way I used to fix on a light in the dark when I was drunk and the room spun. *Control.*

The chairman said something about more sherry and turned from her. She moved, as I knew she would, to find someone else. She would never stand alone in a social circumstance. Her eyes passed over my face and on. And stopped. And came back. They looked at me. They got wider. Her mouth opened and shut. And opened slightly and I saw her take a sharp breath.

I said, "Hello, Jennifer."

"Oh," she said. "Oh."

"It is good to see you again." My voice was steady and calm, far from me, off in some rational distance, proceeding in its rational way.

"Boonie," she said.

"The very one," my voice said.

"Boonie, my God, Boonie." She took my hand suddenly and leaned over and kissed me on the mouth lightly, and pulled back. "Jesus Christ," she said.

I nodded.

"You son of a bitch," she said. "Where have you been?"

"Round the world," I said, "and I'm going again."

"I want to hear," she said, her face now intent upon me, as it had been upon the chairman. "I want to hear about everything."

"I'll be happy to tell you," I said.

"We'll have lunch," she said. "Where are you?"

"Here," I said. "I'm a student."

"My God, so am I."

Her face was a little better than it had been when she was twenty-one. It knew more things. It was not—and the thought squeaked along my nerve lengths—the face of a virgin, for instance. Nor was it, as much as it had been, the face of a child. It contained that same sense of charge, of kinesis, of distilled and radiant femaleness that it had contained when I first saw it, but it had become more elegant.

"Here?" I said. "You're a student here?"

"Yes, I'm working on my M.A. and I have an assistantship. I teach two sections of freshman English."

She was right here. I hadn't been lucky often in the last eight years, but the luck I'd had was mortal. It was luck that Tom Hernandez was hosing down his sidewalk in front of the restaurant. It was luck that Jennifer had gone back to school and here. Where we'd be near, where I had room to work. My hands felt like they were shaking, but I looked at the one that held the sherry and they weren't, they were steady.

She had her hands on her hips and her head cocked looking at me. "Boonie," she said, "you look wonderful. Whatever you've been doing it's certainly been good for you."

"Maybe," I said. "When do you want to have lunch?"

"Tomorrow," she said. "Faculty Club."

"Will they let me in?"

"Are you a teaching assistant?"

"No," I said. "I'm a sophomore."

"Oh, okay. I'll meet you out front. I have a card as a T.A. and a card as John's wife."

"Noon?"

"I'll be there. Boonie, there's so much to talk about."

"I hope so," I said.

CHAPTER
TWENTY-FIVE

I had a studio apartment on Revere Street and that night
I went over my outfit for the next day. I'd never been to a
faculty club. But I'd seen a lot of faculty. My wardrobe
was sufficient. I polished my cordovans, washed and
dried and ironed my chinos, and went over my blue
blazer with Scotch tape to get off any lint there might be.
I had two clean shirts: blue and white. I chose the white
one and put it out on the bureau. Tie selection was easy.
I had a black knit and blue and red rep. I took the rep. I
tucked a pair of dark blue socks into the cordovans, and
put them on the floor at the foot of the bed. Then I stood
back and surveyed, dressing myself in my imagination
and, I realized, making slight indications of the dressing
motions as I went through it: socks, pants, shirt, shoes,
tie, coat. Belt. I had forgotten a belt. I had only one, a
dark brown alligator belt. I got it from the closet and
hung it over the hanger throat where my pants and
blazer were. A pocket handkerchief would be a touch of
class, but I didn't have one. I checked my wallet. It

would be awkward if I couldn't afford the lunch. There were nine dollars in my wallet. I got out the checkbook and wrote a check for cash. I'd cash it at the bursar's office after class. Tomorrow I had a nine and a ten. I'd be free at eleven.

I checked out the wardrobe again, then I got undressed and read *Piers Plowman* until I got too sleepy. Reading *Piers Plowman* does not impede sleepiness. When I put *Piers Plowman* down and turned off the light I was sleepy but I couldn't sleep. I hadn't expected to and I didn't fret. I lay as quietly as I could and kept my mind as empty as I could. I thought about what I'd do if I had all the money I wanted. And what I'd eat if I were to create my absolute perfect menu, and what kind of car I'd drive, and what kind of house I'd buy, and what kind of wardrobe I'd create. I thought about the all-time greatest ballplayers by position (I spent time deciding if Stan Musial would be a first baseman or an outfielder.) The all-time greatest ballplayer poll stopped somewhere in the mid-nineteen fifties because I didn't know anything about the players in the second half of the nineteen fifties. After Jennifer had married John Merchent, I'd lost half a decade. I moved on, listing the ten most desirable women I could think of, but once again those lost years hampered me, and always there was the steady tension that centered in my solar plexus. The night seemed shorter than it should have, had I been continuously wakeful. Morning came.

I brushed my teeth carefully, showered for a long time, and shaved closely, lathering twice and going over it again. I dried my hair by rubbing it with a towel, and toweled the rest of me dry. I sat on my bed, put on my

dark blue socks, stood up, unwrapped the white shirt
from its laundry package, and put it on. I buttoned it
from the top button down, and then put on my pants,
right leg, then left leg. I tucked in the shirttail, smoothing
it all around, and buttoned the pants and zipped the fly. I
slid my belt through the loops and buckled it and lined
up the buckle with the line of my shirtfront and the line
of my fly. Then, using a shoehorn, I slipped into my
shoes, and tied them with one foot on the floor and one
foot resting on the edge of the bed. I tied the tie in a simple four-in-hand knot and shaped the knot after I had
drawn it tight. With my thumb and forefinger I smoothed
the roll in the button-down collar. My hair was dry. I had
a very short haircut so it dried quickly. Looking in the
bathroom mirror, I made a part with my comb and then
brushed the hair. Back out in my bed-sitting room, I took
the blazer off its hanger and slipped into it. I didn't have
many clothes, but what I had were good. The blazer was
all wool with a full tattersall lining.

In the bathroom mirror I tried the jacket buttoned
and unbuttoned and decided I'd arrive with it buttoned
and unbutton it as we sat down. I held a small tietack
against my tie and decided instead to tuck the shorter
end inside the label loop.

I didn't have a topcoat, so I went with no coat and
shivered some waiting for the elevator at Charles Street
Circle. But I'd spent too much time on my appearance to
set it off with an army surplus field jacket. (Not mine.
Mine had disappeared long ago during the years of exile
somewhere west.)

I took notes in my medieval literature course, but
automatically, listening only with my hand and pencil,

and my U.S. history class went by unrecorded. After class
I left my books on a windowsill in Memorial Hall and
cashed my check at the bursar's. I had fifty minutes until
noon. It was too cold to walk outside. So I began system-
atically to pace the corridors in the Student Union, as-
cending the stairs at the end of each corridor and walking
back on the next floor in the other direction. I wanted to
smoke. I hadn't in more than a year. I wouldn't now. I
kept walking. In my head the refrain to the Four Freshman version of "Take the A Train" reiterated without vo-
lition, over and over and over. *Control,* I thought. *Control.
You've been shot at in Korea and you're afraid of this?
Control.* The faculty club was on the top floor of the Student Union. At five of twelve I was waiting outside the
door. In the hall, near the elevator. I knew she'd be late.
She was always late. But I wasn't. And I wouldn't be.

CHAPTER
TWENTY-SIX

Across the table from me Jennifer ate a crouton from her salad. She had always eaten like that. If she were given a plate of peas she'd eat one at a time.

"Have you missed me, Bonnie?" Her gaze was straight at me as she said it.

"Yes," I said.

"There have been a lot of times when I wished you were around," she said. "To talk to. To help. To explain things. You were always so good at that."

I nodded. The dining room was large-windowed and bright with the winter sun. The walls were Wedgwood blue with white trim. The floor was carpeted in beige, and the tablecloths were pink.

"Have you been doing wonderful, exciting things, while you've been gone?" Jennifer said.

I smiled. "I don't know. A lot of what I've been doing since your wedding is a little vague. I was drunk early and often."

She nodded. Her eyes steady on my face. "You were drunk at the wedding," she said.

"That was amateurish," I said. "I got much more professional as I matured. By the time I got west of Chicago I was a major league drunk."

"How are you now?"

"I'm not a drunk anymore."

"Do you want to talk about it?"

"Not that much to say. I worked at different things, moved around the country, ended up down-and-out in L.A., and decided to make a comeback."

The weight of her interest was delicious. I remembered the department chairman yesterday, and all the men I'd seen her talk with. I knew that everyone she spoke with felt this way, but it was still as dulcet and entrancing as if it were only me. And at the moment, it was. She wasn't calculating in that. She really was interested and she really did concentrate on whatever, or whoever, was before her. What I had come to understand in the years of booze and sorrow was that the impact of her personality created in her no sense of obligation. She could entrance people and so she did. It was a power she used neither for good nor evil, but for the simple, unexamined pleasure of its exercise. I came to understand that before I knew I understood it. There was no Eureka, merely one day I noticed that I had known this for a time. She loved being central. There was nothing malign in this, or even selfish. It was simply a need and she fulfilled it with no more thought than one would give to drinking a glass of water. I wondered if there was more. If thirty-year-old Jennifer was different. There would be time to find out.

"How has it been going for you, my love," I said.

She nodded her head repeatedly. "Good, good. I have a daughter, Suzanna—we call her Sue Sue."

"Sue Sue?"

"Yes. It is awfully beach-clubby, isn't it? Her father started calling her that right after she was born. She's almost four now. We waited until John got his degree."

"You been going to school long?"

"No, this is the first year. I was a housewife till then, but I was getting stir crazy." She shrugged. "So John helped me get a teaching assistantship. I love it. After eight years, I just love it."

"And the kid?"

"John's mother looks after her during the day. She and Sue Sue are close and they have servants, of course, too."

"Never thought John would go into teaching," I said.

"No. That is a surprise. His brother went into the bank, but John wanted to be a professor. There's family money, of course. I don't know how people do it who have to live on a professor's salary. But John really enjoys the students. I guess banking never excited him."

"Still in Marblehead?"

"Yes, right next to John's parents."

"How's that work out?"

"Oh," Jennifer shrugged, "not as badly as it might. Margaret, my mother-in-law, is very handy for Sue Sue, and all. She's kind of bossy and full of advice. You know the kind. Often wrong but never uncertain? When we were first married and John was getting his Ph.D. at Harvard she came to our Cambridge apartment one day when we weren't there and rearranged my furniture."

"How's John feel about her?"

"Oh, he says I shouldn't let it bother me. If we disagree, he tries to mediate—he's very reasonable, you know. His field is the eighteenth century. He's always the man of reason. If Margaret and I have an argument, he judges the thing on its merits."

"She's wrong," I said.

"Margaret?" Jennifer looked startled.

"Yeah. If she disagrees with you, she's wrong. You're right. You are much too wonderful to be wrong."

Jennifer laughed her thrilling laugh. "Oh, Boonie. It's good to have you around again. Can we be friends?"

"Sure," I said. "It's one of the reasons I came back."

"Like we were? You really were the best friend I ever had."

"You were that to me," I said.

"And you really were, still are, like nobody else. I still haven't met anyone like you."

"And I was just a kid then," I said. "Wait till you see how much better I've become. You may tear off all your clothes and pounce on me."

"Gee," Jennifer said, "we could never eat at the faculty club again."

The sexual reference made my throat tighten. I had to force my voice out, but it sounded normal enough once out. I thought of her and Merchent waiting before they had the baby, taking precautions, and having intercourse carefully, sleeping together each night, being naked together often. I thought of the casual and intimate possession that people develop when they've been married a few years, a possession that excludes the rest of the world, that sets them apart regardless of their passion for each other, that marks *us* and differentiates from *them*. It was almost too much. It almost overwhelmed me. Almost drove me backward into the despair I'd worked so fiercely at overcoming. For a moment everything swam in front of me, and ran together, and I clasped my hands beneath the table as hard as I could, swelling the muscles in my arms and then my chest and back. *Control.* I had come this far. I was with her. Talking of being friends. I could look at her, and if I reached out and touched her, she wouldn't flinch. "Time is but the stream I go fishing in." The time she's been with Merchent, the kid, the press of nakedness, the life they led, was downstream from where I fished. The stream kept going and the water I fished in was always new. When I had her again, the others who had had her wouldn't matter. Except as obstacles they didn't matter now.

CHAPTER
TWENTY-SEVEN

In a classroom in the science building there were thirteen whites and three Negroes. All the whites except me wore lapel buttons that said HONKIES FOR INTEGRATION. I was for integration, but I wasn't sure that we sixteen were going to get it done.

On the green chalkboard behind the podium at the front of the room someone had chalked a long equation, boxed it in, and written SAVE beside it. The equation was entirely mysterious to me.

A very thin Negro man came in. He was medium height with short hair and a goatee. He wore round gold-rimmed glasses, and carried a cane. He had on a black homburg, a black double-breasted suit with a faint gray pin stripe, a black shirt, and a dark gray tie. He looked down at the three Negroes sitting in the front row and murmured, "Brothers." They murmured back. Then he leaned his cane against the podium, rested his hands against either edge of the top of the podium, and leaned over it toward us.

"My name is Willie Smith and I have been to the belly of the beast," he said. "Before I return there, I want to tell you about it."

He was a spellbinder. He spoke without notes for forty-five minutes of Mississippi, and the voter registration efforts there and the danger that freedom riders faced. The audience was rapt. When it was over they swirled up and to the front of the room and surrounded him. A young black man in a white coat wheeled in a table of tea and coffee and small multicolored sugar cookies, and stood silently behind the table, pouring coffee or tea as requested, and allowing people to help themselves to the cookies.

Jennifer shook Willie Smith's hand. "You were magnificent," she said. "Are magnificent."

Willie said, "Thank you, thank you."

"We are with you," Jennifer said. "We are—" She paused for a moment, trying to express herself just right. One of the three Negroes said, "Who's this we? You talking for all the honkies?"

I had been standing back watching Jennifer, staying out of the way. When he said that I stepped forward, between him and Jennifer. "She's probably talking for herself," I said. "And the people she knows. Are you talking for all the niggers?"

The room became quiet. The awful word was out. I knew they thought it was awful. But I knew that Roy Washington and I used it as commonly as swearing. It depended on how it was used. And since Roy had taught me to box I cared less than I used to about whether people liked what I said.

"You got no right to say something like that," the Negro said.

Willie Smith was looking at me steadily.

"There's three thousand white students in this university," I said. "And thirteen of them showed up here. It's dumb to call one of those thirteen a honkie."

Jennifer put her hand on my arm. "Boonie," she said. "He has more right to be angry than we do."

"Not at you," I said. "Not in front of me."

"The gentleman's right, brother," Willie Smith said. "We won't make no progress 'less we can get together." He looked at Jennifer. "Negroes get touchy after a while, miss," he said. "They get suspicious of white people who say *we* this and *you* that. Tends to underscore the racial split, if you see what I mean."

Jennifer nodded. "Of course."

"It doesn't underscore it as much as a button that says Honkies for Integration," I said.

Willie Smith looked straight at me and the force in his eyes behind the silly gold-rimmed glasses told me something about why he had been to Mississippi and returned. "I agree," he said. "I see you're not wearing one. Even though you're here. I assume you are opposed to racism?"

"Yes," I said.

Smith smiled. "I like that." He put out his hand. "An honest man," he said. We shook hands. "Ask a white man if he's opposed to racism," Smith said to all the audience, "and if he runs on about how much he's opposed and how he hates it and what he'd like to do to stop it, you can be pretty sure you've got a man who feels guilty and probably has reason to." He turned to me. "You don't feel guilty, do you?"

"No."

"Have black friends?"

"I have."

"Some of your best friends?" Smith smiled.

"She's my best friend," I said.

"You ever care to come down to Mississippi and register some black voters, you'll be damned welcome."

"It's a good thing to do," I said. "But I have business here to take care of."

Smith nodded and ate a pink cookie.

When the meeting was over I bought Jennifer a drink across the street at The Basement, a campus hangout on College Avenue.

"He was right, Boonie," Jennifer said. "I was acting as a spokesman for my race. The classic white suburban liberal—oh-my-I-feel-bad-for-you-darkies. God."

"You're not responsible for your upbringing any more than the colored kid was responsible for his. You were sincere. It doesn't matter how you put it."

"But it does," she said. "Language is meaning. The way you say it influences what you say. If we don't believe that, what are we doing here?"

"Here" was actually a small dark bar with pictures of Taft athletes on the wall. But I knew she didn't mean the bar. She meant the university. She meant the study of literature.

"Literature's interesting," I said. "It's good to read, fun to talk about."

"That's all?"

"Yes."

"And racism? Do you care about it?"

"I'm against it," I said.

"But no passion?"

"I think it's the worst thing we've done in this country. It's civilization's worst crime."

She was smoking a Kent cigarette and drinking a small bourbon and water. I knew she wouldn't finish it. She'd sip at it all day if necessary. She didn't like to drink, but she loved the circumstances surrounding drink. Conversation, people, the chance to charm. Now she was interested in me. And in something more than me. Maybe in her. She was trying to talk about something she nearly never talked about. She was trying to talk about how to behave, or she might have been. It was hard to be sure with Jennifer. No one understood her as well as I did. And I didn't understand her all the time. The velocity of her charm, the intensity of her presence made it too dense an experience.

"Is that why you went to that meeting?" she said.

"No."

"Why'd you go then?"

"Because you were going. I enjoy being with you."

"Why'd you come to Taft?"

"Same answer," I said. There was normal hubbub in the bar, but around us a silence seemed to ring. Everything was slowing down the way it does in a car accident, or a fight sometimes. I was aware of my breathing and my pulse.

"Do you believe in God, Boonie?"

"No."

"Do you believe in anything?"

"Yes."

She let some smoke out, pushing her lower lip forward a little so that the smoke drifted up across her face before it thinned.

"What?" she said.

"The answer to that is too corny," I said.

"Tell me."

"I believe in you, Jennifer."

She was silent with the smoke from her cigarette drifting in a thin swirl across her face. Her eyes were large and blue and spaced wide. "Only that?" she said.

"Only that."

"I . . ."

"It's enough," I said.

She put her hand on top of mine. "I've been married eight years, Boonie."

I nodded.

"I have a daughter," she said. "A home, a life."

"That what you believe in?" I said.

She was silent again, looking at the smoke. She shook her head. "I don't think that way, Boonie. I'm very short term. I look for things to do rather than things to believe."

"And you're looking now?"

"Yes," she said.

"Wife and mother's not enough?"

"No."

CHAPTER
TWENTY-EIGHT

As soon as the weather got warm I went to work part time for a carpentry contractor in Cambridge. I took classes in the morning, did framing and some finish work in the afternoon, studied in the evening, and in eighteen months I had a B.A. and twelve hundred dollars in the bank. That fall I was accepted into the graduate program in English at Taft. Because she went only part time, Jennifer was still in the program working on an M.A. and I had caught up with her. I had a teaching fellowship and that entitled me to a desk across from Jennifer's in the teaching fellows' office. We were students together again, and teachers as well. Maybe you couldn't go home again, but you could visit the old neighborhood.

Jennifer and I drank coffee together and talked of Andrew Marvell and the Pearl poet, of Marlowe and Sidney and Dryden and Pope. We argued whether *The Waste Land* was a magnificent failure and whether the new criticism was the only way to approach literature.

We spoke of Cleanth Brooks and Allen Tate and Austin Warren. We never spoke of her husband or her daughter. Every day she rode into school with John Merchent in a Mercedes convertible and every evening she rode home with him.

It was at the department Christmas party that I first actually spoke to him. Jennifer introduced us and drifted off to another group.

"Sure, I remember Boone," Merchent said. He put out his hand. "Good to see you again, Adams."

We shook hands. "Nice to be here," I said.

"I understand you are a master's candidate with us."

"Yes," I said, "I'm a late bloomer."

Merchent smiled. "Never too late," he said. "As Jennifer also demonstrates. You and she have become real chums, it seems."

"Yes," I said. Merchent was still taller than me. Blond, with a smooth face and good clothes. He held himself erect and still, as if the weight of his self-satisfaction gave him an imperturbable ballast.

"We really must get together," he said. "Have you out some Sunday afternoon to drink some beers and chat."

"Yes."

"It's very good for Jennifer, I think, to have a chum like you. She tends to be a bit overwhelmed by some of the demands of university life, and scholarship. In my position I can only help her so much, of course."

"She seems fine to me," I said.

"Oh, surely. She's much better now that she's out of the house and has something to occupy her mind. I'm afraid motherhood and housewifery were not what Jennifer was cut out for."

"She's doing well in class," I said.

"Yes. She's a conscientious student. Probably got some of that from me. When I was doing my book on Teasdale, I had her as what amounts to a research assistant and she learned a great deal about scholarship and research and the standards that scholarship sets."

"Sara Teasdale?" I said.

"Yes. I did the biography of her for the Twayne series."

"You a Teasdale specialist?" I said.

"Well, in a sense," Merchent said. "I have become somewhat of a specialist because no one else has done the research. My critical study of her poetry will be out in the fall, and we're negotiating for a casebook."

"A Sara Teasdale casebook," I said.

"Yes. I was really quite fortunate to find a whole area of literature like that in which little work had been done."

"Did you do your dissertation on her?" I said. He taught the English eighteenth century.

"No, my dissertation was on Nahum Tate," he said. "Let me offer you some advice, Boone. If you're going to publish, it's important to stake out fields of research that haven't been overharvested."

I nodded again.

"Have you developed a special interest yet?" Merchent asked.

"I sure have," I said.

"American or English?"

"American," I said.

He nodded approval. "It's a field that needs some fresh scholarship," he said. "Good seeing you, Adams, let's get together soon, some Sunday afternoon to drink some beers and chat."

"Sure," I said. And Merchent smiled and went to get more sherry and strike up a conversation with the chairman. I looked around. Jennifer, holding a barely sipped plastic glass of sherry, was sitting on the arm of a sofa, listening intently to a young woman explain the problems associated with water fluoridation. The woman wore a white T-shirt and a loose blue denim jumper. She was sitting on the floor with her legs crossed under the skirt. Beside her a young man squatted on his heels. He had on a tan corduroy suit and a plaid flannel shirt with a black knit tie. His hair and beard were untended and long, and his eyeglasses were the kind that the army used to issue, neutral-colored plastic frames with round lenses. I didn't know the girl. The guy squatting beside her was named Allan Raskin. He was writing his doctoral dissertation on Lawrence Ferlinghetti.

"It's an intrusion of my right not to ingest fluoride," the girl in the denim jumper was saying. Her dark hair was long and very curly. "The government has no business medicating me against my will."

Allan Raskin nodded furiously. "Absolutely. There's research that clearly shows fluoride to be poisonous."

"That's not the point," the girl in denim said. "Even if it were perfectly safe, the government has no right to put it in my drinking water. That's a fascist act."

Raskin nodded again. He pointed at her with a shake of his hand. "You're damned right, Trudy. That's a very good point. Even if it's harmless, it's fascist." He nodded again. And kept nodding as if he were following the train of implications even deeper within.

"Are you opposed to chloride too?" Jennifer said.

Trudy shook her head very hard. "No, I won't be sidetracked," she said. "That's a red herring, Jennifer. It's not to the issue. It's exactly the kind of smoke screen they throw up to get our minds off the real issue, which is, and very clearly so, fascism."

Jennifer saw me looking at her across the heads of the anti-fascists. She glanced quickly down at them, saw they weren't looking at her, glanced back up at me, and crossed her eyes. I took a step closer and said, "Excuse me, Jennifer, I'd like to show you something over here if you could give me a minute."

She nodded. "I'll be back, Trudy," she said, and stood up and walked with me to the other corner of the room.

"Thanks," she said. "I have learned more about fascism and crypto-fascism and covert fascism than I ever really wanted to know."

"How come people whose area of specialization and, you'd assume, interest, is literature spend all their time talking about politics?"

"They don't," Jennifer said. "Just the graduate students do that. The undergraduates talk about grades and the professors talk about tenure and promotion."

"Gee," I said. "It's not nearly so platonic as I expected."

"But it's quite a lot of fun," Jennifer said. "Try staying home for three years with a kid."

"It's not like your life has been without adventure

though," I said. "I understand you got to help your husband do his biography of Sara Teasdale."

She looked at me carefully. I kept my face neutral. "One can do a first-rate study of a second-rate figure."

"Sure," I said.

"It's a book, Boonie, and he's got another coming out in the fall. What have you ever written?"

"Nothing much," I said. "I've kept a kind of a journal. I'll show it to you someday."

CHAPTER
TWENTY-NINE

Merchent owned a home on Marblehead Neck with a backyard which, broken by occasional granite outcroppings, sloped down to the water. It was a vast old house done in weathered shingles with a broad veranda all around it. It was furnished in the period when it had been built. There was a lot of Tiffany glass and Victorian furniture. In the front hall an umbrella stand had been made from an elephant's foot. I sat in what Merchent called the back study, with a fire in the fireplace, on a bright October afternoon drinking the second of some beers and having a chat with Merchent and Jennifer and Merchent's mother, Margaret, and, more than I cared to, with his daughter Sue Sue, who was five and a half.

"Of course in class, Boone, and elsewhere in a university context, I would hope you'd call me Dr. Merchent, or Professor Merchent."

"Sure, John," I said.

"You didn't need to tell him that," Jennifer said.

"Better safe than sorry," Margaret said. She wasn't drinking some beers. She was drinking scotch on the rocks and liking it. I could tell. I remembered the feeling, checking the bottle and having that comfortable sense of plenty when you saw it was still almost full. "I always used to tell John's father that. No harm intended, no harm done."

Sue Sue was sprawled on the floor drawing pictures on white paper and scattering them around under our feet. "Here's one of you, Boone," she said.

I looked at the circle with the smile and the round eyes. "Very nice," I said. "May I keep it?"

She nodded and began drawing another one. I said to Merchent, "I was reading a piece by Katharine Balderston recently called 'Johnson's "Vile Melancholy."' What do you think? Is it persuasive to a specialist?"

Merchent's smooth face remained smooth. Then he frowned slightly. "Balderston," he said. Then he shook his head. "I'm afraid I don't know it." He shook his head and smiled. "Departmental business. More and more it interferes with scholarship. Since I became graduate director it's harder and harder to keep up."

Margaret had another scotch on the rocks. "You work too hard as it is, dear," she said.

"Well, the thrust of the thing is that Johnson's melancholy was in fact masochistic. Balderston cites letters . . ."

"Here's another picture of you, Boone," Sue Sue said. It looked much like the other one. Since it was of the same subject I supposed it should. I nodded. "Nice," I said. "Balderston examines letters . . ."

"Aren't you going to keep it?" Sue Sue said.

"No, thank you," I said. "I only have room on my wall for one. I live in a small apartment."

Sue Sue crumpled up the drawing and stomped over to the fireplace and threw it into the flames. Then she made a big sigh and said to Jennifer, "I'm sick of drawing."

"Want to watch TV?" Jennifer said.

"No."

"Come sit on Mamie's lap and draw," Margaret said. "I'd love a picture of me."

"I can't draw on your lap," Sue Sue said. "There's no place for the paper."

Merchent said, "Jennifer, why don't you take her out for a while."

Margaret said, "Oh, no. No. No. The poor thing. She wants to be with all the people. Doesn't she, Sue Sue? She wants to visit with the company too."

"Well," Merchent said, "if you stay, Sue Sue, you have to let us talk, okay?"

"I can talk too," she said.

"But not when someone else is talking," Jennifer said.

Sue Sue got in her grandmother's lap and put her face against her grandmother's shoulder and said, "Nobody likes me."

"Oh, sweetie," Margaret said. She was on her third scotch and was beginning to slush her S's. "Don't be silly, everyone loves you."

"When's he going home?" Sue Sue said.

Jennifer said, "Suzanna!"

Margaret was patting Sue Sue on the back. "She's just tired," she said. "Are you tired, sweetie?"

Merchent sipped his beer from a tall tulip-shaped glass. "I'll have to look into the Balderston article," he said. "Did you happen to see the review of my Teasdale book in J.A.P.A.?"

Sue Sue was continuing to talk against her grandmother's shoulder. "Nobody likes me," she said. "Nobody likes me." The repetition became a kind of chant.

"Mamie loves you," Margaret said. She drank scotch with her free hand. "I'll have just one more drink, dear," she said to John. "Not too much, just one jigger."

"Could you get that for my mother, Jennifer?" Merchent said. Jennifer put down her barely touched bourbon and water and got her mother-in-law's glass and put more scotch in and ice. I noticed she didn't use a jigger.

"You're sure just one jigger, Jennifer?"

"Absolutely," Jennifer said.

"Nobody likes me," Sue Sue crooned. "Nobody likes me."

I said, "I don't recognize the Journal."

"*Journal of the American Poetry Association*," Merchent said. "Very reputable."

Margaret was singing "Rock-a-bye baby, in the treetop" and rocking Sue Sue back and forth. Sue Sue continued to chant "Nobodylikesme nobodylikesme." Neither Sue Sue nor Margaret was very loud. But they were steady.

"Let me get it for you," Merchent said. "It's really a rather interesting piece." He got up and went out of the room. I looked at Jennifer. Her face was bright, intelligent, charming, interested. Her eyes were blank.

"Rockabyenobodylikesmebabyinthenobodylikesmetree top."

The fireplace was made of fieldstone and covered nearly the whole inner wall of the study. Two other walls had bookcases. The rear wall faced out onto the veranda and beyond it down the slope of lawn and rock and garden was the ocean, white-flecked and uneasy. The color of a slate roof.

"Nobodylikesmethecradlewillfallnobodylikesmedown willcomebabycradleandall."

I could feel a small trickle of sweat run down my side from my right armpit. Merchent came back in with his copy of J.A.P.A. open to the review of his critical study of the poetry of Sara Teasdale.

"Let me read it to you," Merchent said. "I'm not sure Mother's heard this yet either." I nodded. I don't know what Jennifer did. I didn't look at her. "'There is real insight,'" Merchent began, "'in Professor Merchent's analysis of the dramatic polarities . . .'"

Margaret continued to sing softly to Sue Sue, who continued to whine softly to Margaret. When Merchent finished reading I said the proper things, glanced at my watch, pretended to be surprised, and said, "Son of a gun. I didn't realize the time. I've got an exam tomorrow."

Jennifer said, "I'll drive you to the train, Boonie," and went to get her coat and mine.

Merchent said, "We'll have to do this more often, Boone," and shook hands.

Sue Sue said, "You got my picture?"

I showed her that I did. Then Jennifer was back and we left.

On the ride to the station I said to Jennifer, "Maybe I should have taken two pictures."

Jennifer said, "It wouldn't have mattered. She'd have

kept drawing until you eventually said no thank you and the rest would have been the same."

"Oh," I said. "That's good, I was feeling guilty."

Jennifer laughed briefly. "Join the group," she said.

CHAPTER
THIRTY

"What do you do for social life, Doonie?" Jennifer said. We were alone in the teaching fellows' office, studying. It was evening and the building was empty except for us and the night cleaning man who shuffled about, dragging his big trash barrel and emptying wastebaskets into it. Jennifer had made us two cups of instant coffee with hot water from the office percolator, and we were taking a break.

"I talk with you," I said. "When I should be studying."

"Besides that?"

"I haven't much time for much besides that. I teach my two sections and grade freshmen compositions—ugh—and take my own classes and study and work weekends as a carpenter. Sometimes I have a couple of beers with the guys I work with."

"No girls?"

I shook my head.

"That's too bad," Jennifer said. "You have a great capacity for affection."

The fist that I kept clenched inside me tightened a little. "Yes," I said. "I do."

We were quiet, sipping coffee. Somewhere, on another floor, a vacuum cleaner hummed. Jennifer's makeup was perfect, her hair exactly in place. She'd been at school since nine o'clock in the morning, but she looked as if she'd just arrived. Her commitment to her appearance was large. As we sat I thought about aging. Neither of us was old, but we looked different than we had. Jennifer's face was more interesting now. There were no lines, no double chins, and yet it was the face of a thirty-six-year-old woman. What had changed?

"You're too closed in, Boonie," Jennifer said. "You're the most entirely autonomous person I've ever met, but you pay a high price for it."

"Not as high a price as I paid when I wasn't autonomous," I said. "When you married Merchent I nearly went under. By the time I bottomed in L.A. a derelict, I was dying. If autonomy means being in control of your life, I had none. Now I do. And I will never lose it again."

It was the first time I'd ever spoken with her in anything but general terms about the bad years. And I found my voice thick with intensity when I spoke of it now. I realized as I heard the intensity how vital my self-control was, how much it meant to me to have dragged myself up out of the bad years. Jennifer heard the intensity too.

"Would you like to tell me about it?" she said.

The vacuum cleaner on the floor above continued. The tone of its hum alternated slightly as it moved forward and backward over the industrial carpeting. Jennifer was leaning forward at her desk, her chin resting on her folded hands.

"Yes," I said. "I would. I can't remember long stretches of it, but I can give you some highlights."

I talked for nearly an hour in surprisingly lucid chronology. The keeping of my journal probably helped the sequence of events in my head, and some of what I told her I remembered from my journal entries rather than from the events themselves.

The vacuum cleaner had gone by the time I finished speaking, and when I finished, the silence was complete. Jennifer had not moved, her enormous eyes steady on my face, her chin still resting on her hands.

"My God," she said.

I was quiet. I felt complicated. There was triumph of a sort; I had finally told her what she'd done to me. But I was embarrassed too, embarrassed that I felt triumph, and embarrassed that I had confessed something shameful. I was risking my control; I had closed the emotional distance between us, and I knew it and it frightened me. I had always fancied myself as one bearing pain with dignity, and this torrential confession seemed antithetical to my fancy.

"How did you stop?" Jennifer said. "What turned you around?"

"I had to have a purpose," I said. "I decided to get you back."

She didn't waver. Maybe she already knew it without exactly saying it. Now, as the words hung between us in the untidy little room, she kept her eyes on me.

"So you stopped drinking, and began the weightlifting," she said, "and the running, and the books?"

"And the nutrition and not smoking and the carpentry and the boxing and the courses and the whole . . ." I searched for a word.

"Self-improvement," she murmured.

"The whole self-improvement," I said.

"For me?"

"If I were going to get you, I had to deserve you."

"For you too," she said.

"Absolutely. It saved me."

Jennifer moved her chin slightly, rubbing it against her hands.

"And now?"

"It continues to save me," I said. "It's what I do. It is my single stay against confusion . . . hell, against dissolution. Without you I would dissipate."

"Still?"

"Still."

"But you're so contained, Boonie. So sure of your integrity, so"—she lifted her chin and spread her hands—"so integrated."

"As long as I can believe in you," I said. "If I can believe in you, I can believe in me. But without you . . . I can find no other purpose in life. It's the difference between love and masturbation. I have to love someone besides myself."

"But you must love yourself too," Jennifer said.

"I was dying," I said. "I needed something to live for. Having someone to love makes life livable, but I think probably I have to be loved back to love myself."

"And it has to be me?"

"Yes."

"Wouldn't it be simpler to fall in love with someone who will love you back?"

"I don't make the news," I said. "I just report it."

"I don't understand that," she said. "I don't understand why you are so centered on me, why you don't find a woman who is single and loving and responsive and everything you want."

"I have chosen you," I said. "I have made a free commitment. There was a woman in L.A. I could have chosen. I didn't. I chose you. I have faith in you. I, by free act of will, love you, and choose always to love you."

Jennifer shook her head sadly. "You want the wrong person," she said. "You don't know me. I'll never be what you want me to be."

I felt the bottom falling out, the blackness beneath. *Control.* I took in a deep breath. *Control.*

"It doesn't matter what you are," I said. "I choose to love you, and I won't choose not to."

"Boonie, I—" She stopped, tightened her mouth, and let her breath out through her nose.

"I know," I said. "There's nothing to say. Just know that I won't quit, and that you can ask me for anything."

"I've always known that," she said.

CHAPTER
THIRTY-ONE

Jennifer and I didn't speak of love again. As long as she took courses, I'd take courses. I was her friend. We went places. In spring of 1968 a group of graduate students had a party in a second-floor walkup off Magazine Street in Cambridge.

"John doesn't feel that it is appropriate for a professor to mingle socially like that with the grad students," Jennifer said.

I nodded.

We were sitting cross-legged on the floor in the living room drinking mulled cider with cinnamon. The stereo was playing something that sounded like the oriental music I used to pick up on the radio in Korea. One string being plucked lethargically.

"I guess they're not having anything to drink," Jennifer said. She wore a lavender dress and beige high-heeled shoes. Her gold earrings were big loops and her lipstick was glossy and her eyes shadowed dark. In her honor I wore my blue blazer and my polished cordovans and my rep tie. Our hostess wore a flowered ankle-length dress and bare feet. Her boyfriend wore sandals and cut-off jeans and a tie-dyed T-shirt. The air was thick with marijuana smoke. Two graduate students sat silently on the couch. The boy in paint-stained jeans and moccasins and a collarless green-striped shirt. The girl had on hiking boots and Swiss army shorts and a blue denim shirt with the sleeves cut off. They moved their heads slightly in what might have been time with the one-stringed noises that came from the stereo.

In front of the couch was a coffee table made from an old cable spool. A big yellow tiger cat uncurled and jumped down from it.

"Hey, Jane," I said to the hostess, "what's the cat's name?"

Jane looked startled, as if I'd just awakened her.

"Hester Prynne," she said.

"Cute name," I said.

She nodded. Jennifer murmured to me, "Boy, you are some conversationist."

"If they had a black lab they'd name it Othello," I said.

"Oh, now," Jennifer said, "they're not so bad."

"Like hell they're not," I said. "They are more predictable than Prussian noblemen. They dress the same, they talk the same, they are cute in the same way, they have the same furniture, the same attitudes. All the women look the same: No makeup, pseudo-proletarian clothes, granny glasses as needed."

"God," Jennifer whispered, "they must think I'm a whore."

"No booze," I went on. "A lot of grass. East Indian zither music or whatever the hell that is. Bookcases made with bricks and boards."

"You're so absolute, Boonie. You're scary sometimes. Hard to live up to."

"I'm thirty-six years old," I said. "I've done a lot of things and I've thought about all of them. Sometime in life you have to stop speculating and start deciding. I've done that."

"You've had more experience than most of us."

"It's not the experience," I said. I wanted her to understand. Maybe I even wanted to instruct her a little. "It's what you do with it. It's what you turn it into."

"Why turn it into anything," Jennifer said. "Why does it have to be systematized?"

"So you won't kick around like a grasshopper on a hot afternoon," I said.

Our host in the tie-dyed T-shirt said, "Boone, you were in the army."

"Yes."

He shook his head. They had been talking about Vietnam.

"How'd you let them get you?"

I'd had the conversation before. I knew how it would go. It was like talking sex with a virgin. I sighed softly. Jennifer looked at me.

"They were going to get somebody," I said. "I didn't see any reason why it shouldn't be me."

Jane said, "Wow, they had you brainwashed, didn't they?"

"A different time," I said. "For a lot of us then it was a rite of passage. Now resisting it is a rite of passage."

"That's all you think the antiwar movement is?" the host said.

"Barry," I said, "I don't think about movements any more than I have to. Trying to assign a single motive to a movement is like trying to catch minnows in your fist."

"It's that attitude that permits it," Barry said. "People that don't concern themselves. Easy for you, Boone, I suppose. They can't draft you."

I smiled at Jennifer. "At least I understand that," I said to her. "I can identify with not wanting to get drafted."

"That's a legitimate concern, Boonie," Jennifer said.

Barry was inflamed. "That's not it," he said. "That's not where it's at. That's not what it's about. Our commitment is to change. The world's gone too long this way, the masses like cattle herded into the military to be massacred in wars of imperialism. People who serve in a war are traitors and it's themselves they betray."

For the first time since 1961 I felt like I needed a drink. "*Mea culpa*," I murmured.

"It's Standard Oil that wants this war. It wants the oil in southeast Asia."

I could feel myself going. "Standard Oil isn't anybody," I said. "It's like the peace movement. It's an artificial entity made up of lots of people who are not entirely interchangeable."

"Boone, that's an incredibly naive view of society," Barry said.

I nodded. Jennifer put her hand on my arm.

"Some of the sons of some of the people who work for Standard Oil are at this moment getting their balls blown off in Vietnam," I said. "I don't suppose their parents are fully consoled by corporate profits."

Jane leaned forward, her hands clasped in her lap. "Boone. It's hard for you to understand, I know. It's hard for you to oppose the war. You're older and . . ." She hesitated, trying to think how to say it. "Well, look at you, I mean you lift weights and . . ." She let the rest hang.

"Despite having a thick neck," I said. "I think the war is wrong. I think it's a mistake. But I'm not sure everyone involved in it is evil. I'm not even sure the world would run better if you took it over, Barry."

Barry shook his head with dogged passion. "Things can change," he said. "And people willing to make the commitment can change them."

"I can agree with that," I said. Jennifer sipped at her mulled cider and watched me over the rim of the glass. I smiled at her. "And I believe in commitment," I said.

CHAPTER
THIRTY-TWO

Cambodia had been invaded. Jennifer had marched in protest, and the march had culminated with a takeover of the Student Union Building at Taft. I went with her. I had no sense that we would bring the warmongers to their knees. But Jennifer was passionate about it and I was happy to be with her, to share her passion, or to insert myself in the path of nightstick or firehose if the chance appeared, if I was lucky.

So we sat together on the stairs of the Union while outside the campus police awaited the arrival of the Tac cops. The electricity had been shut off to discourage us, but it merely added to the excitement. Looking back now, I marvel at how every step the authorities took to combat the demonstrations added to the fun of the demonstrations, nourished the demonstrators, enriched their opportunity to demonstrate their authenticity, offered them the consolations of martyrdom and simple joys of nonfatal combat.

"This is crazy," Jennifer said. "You being here. You aren't committed to this."

"I'd like to see them stop the war," I said.

"But that's not why you're here."

"No."

We spoke in whispers, sitting in the dark with students all around us whispering among themselves, and the smell of grass and cigarettes and humanity seeping around us in the close dark. Through the glass doors of the Union there was movement in the quadrangle, but we couldn't see of what. There was the familiar revolving flash of the police cars, but they had been there since we'd occupied the building.

In the dimness, close to me, I could see Jennifer shake her head. "I spend more time with you than with my husband," Jennifer said.

"Yes."

"He should be here with me."

"Or you with him," I said.

"He doesn't approve of this; he wants to become chairman of the department."

"His wife's behavior would have some effect on that," I said.

"Well, it shouldn't. I'm who I am, he's who he is."

"True," I said. "But it does. Probably always will."

"You would say the hell with being chairman."

"To be with you," I said.

I could feel her left thigh pressed against mine. Her hip. Her left arm and shoulder. We had to lean close to hear each other's whispers.

"Are we being silly, Boonie?"

"You and me?"

"No, all of us. All of us who march and protest and occupy buildings and try to change things?"

"No, you're not silly," I said. "It's bound to help. It already has."

"Sometimes I feel like a jerk," Jennifer said. "A grown woman marching around with a bunch of kids yelling slogans. John says I should grow up."

"This is one of the ways," I said

"Yes," Jennifer said. "Yes, it is. John says I am selfish, that I've abandoned my responsibilities and been swept up in myself. He says all I care about is being with it."

"You don't believe him," I said.

"Partly. Partly he's right. I am selfish. I care about myself. Maybe I'm learning to care about myself more than about anything else. Maybe I am caring too much. But I'm finally important. I'm finally involved in the world and people take me seriously. Can you understand that?"

"Sure," I said. "Among other things, this is a way to be taken seriously. There's some risk. Risk is the earnest money of conviction. Most of the people in here are after what you're after."

"But most of them are kids," she said.

"So we age more slowly than some," I said.

"You're not like me," Jennifer said. Close to her on the stairs I could see her smile again. "Or the other kids. You don't need to do this."

"Not for the same reasons," I said.

"You do this for me," Jennifer said. "You grew up a long time ago."

It was thrilling to talk with her about myself. It was too exciting for me. It threatened my control. But it was irresistible. I wanted her to go on.

"In some ways you're right," I said. "I grew up in the years after I bottomed out in L.A., and I had to learn what mattered. I'm clear on that now. I know what I care about. I know what I need to control and what I can control and what I can't. It's a kind of freedom."

Outside, a man with a bullhorn told us we'd have fifteen minutes to clear the building and then we'd be subject to arrest. A stir of near-sexual excitement ran through the kids massed there in the dark.

"What do you need to control, Boonie?"

"Me. My feelings. I feel very strongly. If I don't keep them clamped all the time, they run to excess. They're destructive of me and other people. If I combine them with drink, it's a mess."

"Humor," Jennifer said.

"It's one way," I said. "It's a distancing trick. Another way is to stay inside."

"Inside yourself," Jennifer said.

"Yes."

The word passed among the kids in the dark. *Link arms.* I put my arm through Jennifer's. The phrase moved through the crowd like the domino effect. *Link arms.*

"And in college," Jennifer said. "When I called you and asked you to rescue me from Nick?"

"I took the leash off," I said. "Or if you prefer a different metaphor, I let you inside."

In back of us, up the stairs, someone began to sing "The Battle Hymn of the Republic." The bullhorn announced ten minutes. The song spread, like the link arms had spread before it, tying people together. Everyone stood.

"And so," Jennifer was whispering close to me, "when I turned away from you, you took to drinking and the unleashed emotions nearly killed you."

"Dramatic," I said.

"There you go, distancing again."

I nodded.

"I never understood exactly," Jennifer said. "Maybe I can't even now. I don't have the same emotions you do. They've never been in need of control, I suppose. Or maybe they're under such control that it's a way of life. Either way I never quite understood how betrayed you must have felt."

The lights came on suddenly. The bullhorn announced, "*Five minutes.*" Jennifer's eyes widened as they came on and she thought of something. "Maybe still feel," she said.

"No," I said. "I'm beyond that. That way madness lies."

The crowd inside the Student Union, on its feet, arms linked where possible, singing now lustily, waited in ominous sensuality. Outside the bullhorn sounded again. A bored mechanical voice, "You are trespassing. If you do not leave the premises of the Student Union in two minutes, you will be forcibly removed and subject to arrest."

The singing grew lustier. Jennifer's face was bright with excitement. Her hair was beautifully done. Her jewelry expensive, her eyeshadow flawless, her lips were parted and her teeth were very white. Occasionally she rubbed the tip of her tongue on her lower lip. I felt as if I might burst, like the ancient Greek fertility god. But what I felt wasn't hubris. It was love and it nearly over-powered me.

"When the cops come, stay close to me," I said.

Jennifer looked at me with the excitement gleaming in her face. "I can take care of myself," she said.

"I know," I said. "I was hoping you'd take care of me."

CHAPTER
THIRTY-THREE

On a June morning Jennifer and I went to the cellar of the Chapel Building at Taft to dig up our Ph.D.s. The diplomas were in cardboard boxes in which copy-machine paper had originally been shipped. Two undergraduate girls were in charge.

"We've come," I said, "to receive our degrees."

"Names?" one of the girls said.

We gave them. The girls shuffled through the boxes and found the diplomas, bound in red leather with TAFT UNIVERSITY in gold on the cover. The girl who'd asked for our names brought them to us. As she held them out she rendered a brief excerpt of the traditional graduation march, "Dah, da da da dah da."

Afterward, holding the diplomas, we walked along the Charles River.

"Think how smart we are now," I said.

"Yes," Jennifer said, "dumb no more."

"Should we celebrate?" I said.

"Yes, we should. I actually am very proud to have

done this. When I went to college it was so that I could become educated and marry a man with a white-collar job. An educated woman was more interesting at cocktail parties and having dinner with the boss."

A college crew swept by on the river, the oars moving in muscular unison, the coach following in a small red speedboat yelling instructions through a megaphone.

"I got my B.A. for somebody else," Jennifer said. "But the Ph.D. was for me."

"If nothing else," I said, "it certifies endurance."

Jennifer nodded. "It's more," she said. "It means I can proceed as Jennifer Grayle instead of Mrs. John Merchent."

"It's the way I prefer to think of you," I said.

She smiled. "The Ph.D. is certification. But in fact, I may have learned more from you, Boonie, than I did from the Ph.D. In a way, you've brought me up. I had a chance to see in you things I see in no one else. You remain what you are. You are true to yourself."

I smiled. Jennifer shook her head impatiently.

"I know that's a cliché, true to yourself, but I don't care. You are. You don't betray what you are because you want something from someone or you are afraid of someone. Most men I know, and women, really do lead lives of quiet desperation. You don't. Because you don't I know that it's possible not to."

I knew if I pointed it out to her she'd see the irony of that, that she'd remember that my life was a single-minded desperation. But it would have led us to an area we tacitly avoided, an area too uncertain for us, where I, as much as she, feared the terrain and the consequences. So I nodded and shrugged. I knew what she meant. In a sense she was right. My one consuming desperation eliminated all others. Caring only for her, I was free to care about nothing else.

"You taught me by being with me, Boonie, and by being what you are. And by being . . ." Jennifer seemed briefly to search for the right word. Then she made a small laugh. "I'm so taken with my new intellectual eminence that I'm searching for original phrases. The hell with it. What I mean is that you are completely steadfast. Watching you manifest that has been of more service to me than I can say."

"This should probably all be saved for Valentine's Day," I said. "But I have learned as much from you as you ever did from me. I've learned that my definitions, my rules, my certainties, are not universal, that feeling something strongly doesn't make it right. You are good, and when you do things that I wouldn't do, they can't be bad. They can only be different."

We stopped walking and Jennifer turned toward me and we looked at each other.

"Each of us seems to have been able to offer just what the other needed," she said.

Beyond the point where we stood the river turned and deepened, flowing under trees that darkened its surface. As the channel narrowed and the water hastened in its rush, twigs that had floated placidly past us began to dance upon the surface, tossed by the compressed energies beneath them.

"Yes," I said. "I have noticed that too."

CHAPTER
THIRTY-FOUR

I had begun to excerpt small pieces from my journal and polish them and send them out to small intellectual magazines that paid you in free copies. The magazine published several of them and I was encouraged. They were not stories really, they were small, fragmentary set pieces whose meaning, if there was any, resided in the language itself. One reviewer called them sketches and said that my style was "spritely though not without error."

Jennifer's doctoral dissertation, *Jane Austen and the Function of Being Female,* was published, slightly revised, by the Wesleyan University Press and got some rather good reaction in the scholarly journals. Some of the feminist press liked it too, but some found it lacking in doctrinal purity.

"It's what you get for using big words," I said. We were having coffee in the faculty section of the Taft student cafeteria. Jennifer smiled.

"I don't like it, Boonie. I hate being criticized."

"Who likes it?"

"You've had criticism on those sketches you published. You don't seem to mind."

I shrugged. "It's publish or perish," I said. "If they keep me from perishing, I am willing to take some intellectual abuse in journals of limited circulation."

"But it must make you angry sometimes, or hurt your feelings."

"At a low level," I said. "But not very deeply and not very long. I didn't write it for them, you know? I like what I write. If you like it too, it's unanimous."

She shook her head. Around us the students ate and studied and read *The Boston Globe*. The smell of coffee and steam-table food dominated the other smells: tobacco, perfume, the disinfectant soap that they mopped the floors with. The noise was mostly boisterous student sounds. Profanity, the current phrases, the occasional blare of a portable radio. The service was mostly Styrofoam and plastic, so there was little of the clatter that you often hear in a cafeteria.

"That would never be enough for me," Jennifer said. "Just your approval and my own. I need a larger audience. I need to be liked and admired by a lot of people." She paused and sipped her coffee. "In fact, I tend to get angry at people who don't like me or people who don't like what I do. I hate disapproval and I am inclined to take it personally."

"Forewarned is forearmed," I said. "I think you're never wrong."

"Never?"

"Well, hardly ever. I didn't fully approve of that Dear John you sent me in Korea."

A busboy in a white coat pushed a clean-up cart among the tables, cleaning off the napkins and Styrofoam cups and plastic spoons and torn wrappers from sugar and Sweet 'n Low. At our table he stopped and swept our unfinished cups into his plastic trash and wiped the table clean with a damp towel. Jennifer and I looked at each other. The kid moved on, oblivious to us.

"Seemed a little late to protest," I said.

"Boy's probably preoccupied with other things," Jennifer said.

"Musing," I said, "passionately on the potential for scoring some grass after work."

I went and got two more cups for us and brought them back to the table. Jennifer was looking at her lecture notes. She had that capacity to work in three-minute bursts if need be, to accomplish something in the smallest of time frames. I couldn't. I needed long, uninterrupted stretches. She smiled at me when I put the coffee down.

"You know," she said. "I'm not sure I was wrong to break up with you back then. Isn't that a lovely quaint phrase from the past? 'Break up with.' The person I was might not have been able to do it. I was sort of scared of you. You had so much passion and it was so fierce. You were so moral, so insufferably honorable, so needy. It put a great deal of pressure on me. I wasn't like that. I'm still not like that. But I'm beginning to be able to feel good about what I am. I'm not like you and I don't mind. But back then, I don't know. In secret I felt, maybe I wasn't even clear on it myself—it's not my kind of introspection, especially then—that you were a kind of implicit criticism of my own failures."

I nodded.

"You were—you know this—the first person I ever knew who had a code of behavior. I didn't even know people had them except in fiction. Real people simply did what they could to get what they wanted. So when I encountered you and you had actual views on right or wrong which were not rooted in being popular or getting a date for the ATO house party, I thought it must be the only code. If I weren't like you I must be bad."

"I kind of thought that myself," I said.

"So if I'd married you I might have been miserable. You might have been miserable too. We might have made each other miserable."

"I was pretty miserable without marrying you," I said.

"That's where those sketches come from, isn't it?" she said.

"Yes. I kept a journal, and I've been mining it."

"A journal?"

"Yes. All through it. Even entries that I don't remember making. Thirteen spiral notebooks."

"When do they stop?"

"They haven't stopped," I said. "They are ongoing. They began when you started returning my letters. After a while I started writing and not mailing."

There was complication in Jennifer's face. I didn't recognize all of it, but puzzlement was there, and something stubborn.

"I won't feel guilty about that," she said.

I drank some coffee. It had the taste it always had when you've drunk too much. It didn't really taste good.

Low-level addiction. Or habit. I wondered if habits were addictive.

"What are you going to do with it, Boonie?"

"The journal?"

Jennifer nodded.

"Eventually," I said, "I will probably edit it down into a novel, or maybe several. In the meanwhile I will pluck out some quick publications so they'll give me tenure."

"I'd like to read it," Jennifer said. Her coffee grew cold in front of her. It often did. When she became interested in something, anything, it was nearly exclusive. She leaned toward me a little and her wonderful face was serious and interested and thrilling. Her voice was wonderful too, full of unimaginable possibility.

"The whole thing?" I said.

"Yes. It's not just curiosity. I'm a good editor, maybe I can help."

"Work on it together?" I said.

"Yes."

My life's work, now shared with my life's purpose. I was flooded with ecstasy. It was hard to breathe except in small, shallow gulps. Art and life unified, or almost. I clenched against the vertigo. *Control.*

"Sure," I said. "I'll bring it in tomorrow."

CHAPTER
THIRTY-FIVE

Jennifer sat with me in my office with one of the journals spread open between us on my desk, and the rest of
them in a large cardboard box that said on the side
ROLLING ROCK.

She shook her head a little. "They are . . . they are
simply remarkable, Boonie, they are . . ." She hunched
her shoulders a little and shook her head again. "I understand you. I don't think I've ever read anything that so
fully articulates . . ." She hunched her shoulders again
and held them hunched while she searched for the proper
phrase. Then she let them drop in a kind of resignation.
"I understand you."

"But do you respect me," I said.

She smiled. "I respect you like hell," she said.

"Do you remember the circumstances when we saw
Nichols and May?"

"Yes," Jennifer said. "You were on your first leave
from basic training and I met you in New York. You
didn't even have civilian clothes."

"In a way it's like thinking about other people," I said, "like thinking about our children. We slept together in the same room at the Biltmore and we didn't have sex."

"You thought it would be ignoble," Jennifer said. "I was afraid I'd get pregnant."

"What do you think I have to do to make this journal into literature?"

"It's hermetic," Jennifer said. "It is entirely internal. It might have all taken place in a cave as far as connecting with the larger world is concerned."

"Yes. It's just you and me."

"No. It's just you, I'm in there only as I impinge on you. There needs to be more. Not necessarily more of me. More of life. More landscape. More chronical."

I nodded.

"The way you are is not common, but it must be human. I'd like to see us connect it some way to other human experiences, so that a person reading it could say, 'Yes, yes, that's right.'"

"You seem to be suggesting a lot of work," I said.

"Yes," Jennifer said, "a lot. But it's not more work than we can do."

"There isn't anything that is more than we could do."

"I know."

"You make me better than I could be alone. I am more than my own sum, with you."

"I know, Boonie. You have done that for me. I am much more than I could have been if you hadn't come back."

"That's not my doing," I said. "That's yours."

"I deserve credit," Jennifer said. "I've become almost

a whole other person, and I'm proud to have done it. I had gone back to school before you returned. But once you returned you embodied possibility."

"Lazarus," I said.

"Yes. Rebirth was possible. And more, you were someone who would always approve of . . . no, that's wrong. You wouldn't always approve. And you shouldn't. That's nursery-school gobbledygook. You were someone who was absolute. You were certainty. Approve or disapprove, you were irrevocably mine. Whatever I did would not change you; the world would not change you."

"You were right," I said.

"Yes. I know. I always knew. Even when I married John I knew that he wasn't the one I could count on. You were. It made life more possible. It was a certainty. As I grew older I found there were no other certainties."

"So how come you married John?" We were in the midst of the afternoon. Students wandered up and down the corridor outside my office door, keeping appointments with professors, keening over grades, and puzzling over comments in the margins. From the main office there was the sound of typewriters and the mimeograph machine and the photocopy machine. But in my office the silence seemed to spiral back down a dwindling quarter-century as I asked, out loud, for the first time, the question to whose drumbeat I had stepped since 1954.

"You wanted all of me, Boonie. Not just to love me, to own me. To possess me, to own my soul, to own all of me. I don't think I quite knew it then. But now I do, and one way that I do is because now you love me. Just love me. Don't wish to hold me in vile duress. Now you can trust me, and so now I can trust you."

"You've made me whole," I said.

She shook her head. "The commitment made you whole. Even if we were never to be lovers you'd be whole."

"Ever wilt thou love," I said. "And she be fair."

She nodded. "Something like that."

"But if we were never lovers, I wouldn't be happy," I said. "I would always want to be."

"But you'd be whole."

I nodded.

Jennifer's face was steady on mine. I listened to the sound of my breath going in and out. I heard myself swallow once.

"Nineteen fifty-four was too early," Jennifer said. "Neither of us was whole then." I could feel myself rocking slightly in my chair, volitionless, thick with silence, faintly dizzy. Jennifer got up and went to the office door and closed it and turned and looked at me and said, "Now we are."

CHAPTER
THIRTY-SIX

I stood. The sound of my breath quivered in the crystalline space between us. Jennifer stood with her back against the door, her palms flat against the door on each side of her hips. The smell of her perfume was enveloping.

"I didn't know I was going to say that today," she said.

I didn't move.

"Do you want me?" she said.

I nodded.

"Do you want me to leave John and live with you?"

I nodded.

"And when I divorce him do you want to marry me?"

Nod.

"I think you should kiss me now," Jennifer said.

I put my hand on my desk and held myself steady. My breath was short. I was breathing through my mouth and each exhalation made a little *huff*. I tightened my grip on the edge of the desk and felt the muscles in my forearm clench. My eyes were full of tears.

Jennifer made a small nod with her head and stepped to me and put her arms around me and kissed me on the mouth and I felt myself unclench, and my spirit burgeoned, spread throughout me and mingled with her perfume and her heat and the weakness was gone and I pressed her against me with the unbestowed strength of a silent quarter-century feeling her press back and feeling my soul begin at last to romp with hers in newly created pastures where eternity shimmered before us and time, just begun, was ours forever.

EPILOGUE

. . . with my body I thee worship, with all my worldly goods I thee endow.